I0662975

THE GUNSMITH

473

Freakville

Books by J.R. Roberts
(Robert J. Randisi)

The Gunsmith series

Gunsmith Giant series

Lady Gunsmith series

Angel Eyes series

Tracker series

Mountain Jack Pike series

COMING SOON!
The Gunsmith
474 – Outlaw's Gun

For more information visit:
www.SpeakingVolumes.us

THE GUNSMITH

473

Freakville

J. R. Roberts

SPEAKING VOLUMES, LLC
NAPLES, FLORIDA
2021

Freakville

Copyright © 2021 by Robert J. Randisi

All rights reserved. No part of this book may be reproduced or transmitted in any form or by any means without written permission.

ISBN 978-1-64540-541-2

Chapter One

Clint Adams had to admit his interest had never before been captured the way it was by the road sign that announced: TOWN OF FREAKVILLE, Pop. XXXXX. The numbers had been crossed off, so there was no telling what the population might be. Still, he'd ridden through many towns with less curious names.

However, his interest had been piqued even before he reached Freakville. He had gone only a few more miles when he saw the wagon in the middle of the road, leaning to one side because of a broken wheel.

He reined in behind it, heard somebody on the other side who was obviously working on the wheel.

"Need some help?" he asked.

"I got it," a voice answered.

Clint strained to see who had spoken but couldn't find anyone.

"We'd get it fixed faster with two of us working," he offered.

"I said I got it," the voice said again. It was an odd, rather high-pitched voice, but not a woman or a child.

"Why not let him help, Bizzy?" This voice sounded like a woman. "We'd get done faster."

A woman stuck her head out the back of the wagon and smiled at Clint. She had a moon face that hinted at extra weight, but very pretty eyes.

"Bizzy likes to do things himself," she told Clint.

"Bizzy?" Clint still couldn't see anyone else.

"My name is Bartholomew," the odd voice said, and then an equally odd creature appeared from the other side of the wagon. "This would go a lot faster if you'd get that fat ass of yours out of the wagon," he shouted up to the woman.

The speaker was a little man of about three-and-a-half feet tall, with a bulbous nose and tufts of red hair over each prominent ear.

"Well," the woman said, "now that there's a real man here, maybe he can help me down."

"It'd be my pleasure, Ma'am."

Clint dismounted and approached the wagon. The extra weight that the woman's face had hinted at was nothing compared to what he saw as more of her appeared. She put a hand out for him to assist her, and he was worried that he might crumple beneath her more than three-hundred pounds.

She stepped down using her other hand to hold onto the wagon, and together they got her feet on the ground. She was wearing a dress that extended down to her ankles but showed off her shoulders and upper breasts.

She had the smoothest looking skin he had seen in a long time. On top of that, her fragrance was heady.

"Thank you, kind sir," she said. "My name is Emmeline—Emmy, for short. That's my husband, Bartholomew, although everybody calls him Bizzy. He does a lot of odd jobs around town."

"The town of Freakville?" he asked.

"That's right," she said. "As you can see, we belong there."

"Maybe you're a freak," Bizzy said, "I ain't." He looked at Clint and stuck his jaw out. "You gonna help me, or what? We gotta get this wheel up off the ground so I can repair it."

"Oh, yeah, sure," Clint said. "Why don't you just tell me what you want me to do."

With Bizzy shouting orders, they managed to get the busted wagon hiked into the air, after which Bizzy did an amazing job of temporarily fixing it so they could get back to town.

"Great job," Clint said, as they settled the wagon back down on the ground.

"Yeah, well, Emmy's gonna get back in it, so it'll probably break again before we get back."

"I'd walk," Emmy said, spreading her fat arms, "but as you can see, I'm not really built for it."

"Well," Clint said, "let me help you back into the wagon."

Helping her climb back in was more of a chore than getting her out, had been. Bizzy gave Clint a mighty glare as he was forced to place one hand squarely on Emmy's butt to push her into the wagon.

Once she was inside, she managed to turn around and stick her head out, again.

"Why don't you follow us into town?" she invited. "The least we can do is give you a good meal and a place to stay."

Clint could tell from the look on Bizzy's face that he wasn't happy about the invitation, but he said to Emmy, "I accept. Thanks."

Clint thought about offering to help Bizzy get up in front of the wagon but decided against it. As he watched, the little man climbed up very easily. Despite his size, he seemed strong and agile. He picked up the reins, snapped them and got the two horse team moving. Clint mounted up and followed.

Chapter Two

Clint followed the wagon for a few miles until they reached what looked like the remnants of a town. Many of the buildings were at least partially collapsed, some had been patched up with canvas, so that they looked like half building and half tent.

As he followed the wagon down the main street, he realizes that the name of the town was not only due to Emmy and Bizzy's presence. He saw a man who seemed to be seven-feet-tall and rail thin; another man who appeared to have nails coming out of his face; a bearded lady; two people who looked to be connected at the hip; and a half dozen other oddities, all of whom were staring at *him* as if he were the odd one.

Bizzy drove the wagon to a large tent that had been erected at the far end of town. It looked to Clint like what was called a "big top" in the circus.

Once inside, several had appeared to help Emmy down from the wagon. Bizzy climbed down with amazing agility.

"Go ahead and dismount," Emmy invited. "We can have someone see to your horse, and then get you fed and housed."

Clint dismounted and a rather normal looking man came over to take the reins.

"Fine animal," he said. "We got a stable out back. I'll take good care of him."

Clint took his saddlebags and rifle from the horse, and then allowed the Tobiano to be led away. The people he had seen in town might have been odd, but he didn't feel threatened in any way.

Two other men began to unhitch the team from the wagon.

"We got things to do," Bizzy said to his wife.

"We have a guest," she countered. "I'm gonna get him somethin' to eat and introduce him to the Count."

Bizzy spit on the ground and walked away.

"He doesn't like me," Clint said.

"He doesn't like anyone taller than him," she said, then giggled. "That means everybody. Come on. You look hungry. We have a mess tent."

He followed Emmy as she waddled out of the tent. Outside, he caught up to her and walked alongside.

"Who's the Count?" he asked.

"He's the ringmaster," she said. "That is, he was the ringmaster when he was with the circus."

"Is everyone here from the circus?" he asked.

"Circus, carnival," she said. "We were all performers once."

"What happened?"

"Most of the outfits we were with went bust," she said. "We can't all be working for P.T. Barnum, or Cooper and Bailey's circus."

"Cooper and Bailey?"

"Barnum's biggest competitor, for a while, until they joined forces to become Barnum and Bailey."

Clint had met Barnum years ago in New York, when the man gave him his Darley Arabian, Eclipse, but he hadn't seen him in many years. The man had gone on to major success.

"So how did you end up here?"

"The Count found this ghost town and decided to take it over. He started inviting those of us who were out of work."

"Why name it Freakville?"

"Because we're all freaks," she said, "and not ashamed of it."

"Why Arizona?" Clint asked.

"Who knows?" she said. "Somehow the Count ended up here."

"How many people live here?"

"These days?" she said. "Fifty, maybe sixty. They come and go. Those of us who stay will eventually become part of the Count's show."

"And when will that be?"

"None of us know," she said. "That'll be up to the Count."

She walked him to the mess tent, a smaller version of the "big top" tent they had driven the wagon into. As they entered, he could smell the food, and his stomach growled.

"Grab a plate and get in line," she told him. "We got good cooks, here."

"More than one?"

"They alternate," she told him.

"Aren't you going to eat?" he asked, as she started away.

"I wanna find the Count," she said, "and introduce you."

He looked over at the line of people waiting for food.

"Is it okay for me to eat?" he asked. "I mean, nobody's going to object?"

"We feed strangers passin' through all the time," she said, "but I'll let them know."

She went over to the front of the line and spoke with the older woman who was dishing out the food. She glanced over at Clint and nodded. Emmy waved at him to get in line, and he did. Then she waddled out of the tent.

Clint stood in line behind another small man, though not as small as Bizzy. This one was over four feet, but just barely. Behind him was a tall man who seemed incapable of not smiling.

"Food's gonna be good," the man said.

Clint wanted to ask him how he could do that, talk and keep such a wide smile on his face. His face looked like rubber.

"That's what I've been told," Clint said.

Chapter Three

The food was a simple stew, and it was delicious. There were several wooden tables available where people could sit and eat. Clint sat at one alone, but that didn't last as the man with the rubber smiley face soon joined him.

"You mind?" he asked.

"Not at all," Clint said.

The man sat right across from him.

"This is Aggie's stew," the man said. "It's my favorite, but I can't let Molly know."

"Molly?"

"She's the other cook," the man said. "She and Aggie take turns."

"Ah."

The man proceeded to shovel the stew into his rubber smiley face.

"Oh, sorry," he said. "My name's Jack—Smilin' Jack. You can probably figure out why."

"I think I guessed."

"The fact is," Jack said, "I got precious little to smile about."

Clint was waiting for a "but," only it never came. Smilin' Jack went back to eating. Clint decided not to ask any questions and went back to his own plate.

He had just finished eating when Emmy appeared in the tent again, this time accompanied by a tall man in a black suit. He had slick black hair, a thin mustache, and an authoritative air that filled the tent. He nodded and exchanged greetings with people as he walked past their table.

"Here he is, Count," Emmy said, smiling at Clint. "You know, I never asked you for your name."

Clint stood up and said, "Clint Adams."

"Mr. Adams, meet the Count," Emmy said.

Clint stood and extended his hand.

"Count."

"Mr. Adams," the Count said, accepting his hand. "The Gunsmith?"

"That's right."

"The Gunsmith!" Emmy blurted.

The Count looked at her.

"Emmy I'd like to talk to Mr. Adams alone."

"Oh, sure, Count," Emmy said. "See you later, Mr. Adams."

"Just call me Clint."

"Later, Clint," she said, and waddled off.

"Have a seat, Mr. Adams," the Count said.

Clint sat across from Smilin' Jack.

"Jack?" the Count said.

The smiling man looked at him, then got the message.

"Yes, sir." he grabbed his plate and moved to another table.

The Count sat across from him in the chair Smilin' Jack had just vacated.

"How does he do that with his face?" Clint asked.

"He's a rubber man," the Count said.

"Rubber?"

The Count nodded.

"He can stretch his body in incredible ways."

"But his face . . ."

"Well, he's been doing it so long he can't get that smile off his face," the Count said. "It's stuck there."

"That's amazing," Clint said.

"Most of these people are amazing," the Count said.

"And they're all here because of you," Clint said.

"Yes."

"And they all call you . . . the Count?"

"They do."

"But your name is . . .?"

The man smiled.

"Just the Count."

"Is that . . . an alias?"

"It's more of a title," the man said. "As I understand, you're quite an amazing man, yourself."

"Am I?"

"Well, I mean, with a gun," the Count said. "You're supposed to be fast and accurate."

"I generally hit what I shoot at," Clint said.

"Look," the Count said, "I'm putting together a show, and I could use you—and I mean, as a headliner."

"A headliner?"

"Top of the bill," the Count said.

"And I'd be doing what?"

The Count made a gun out of his thumb and forefinger.

"Hitting what you aim at."

"I never aim," Clint said. "That's a mistake a lot of people make. I just point."

"Well, then," the Count said, "hitting what you point at."

"When does this show start?"

"I'm still working out the details," the Count said.

"And everybody here is waiting?"

"They all want to be part of it."

Clint looked around at the people in the tent-oddities, all of them.

"I'd have to think about it," he said.

Chapter Four

After the Count left the tent, Emmy reappeared, moving faster than Clint had seen before. She rushed to him and sat down.

"I didn't know you were the Gunsmith!" she blurted.

"My fault," he said. "I didn't introduce myself."

"Can I still call you Clint?"

"Of course."

"When I brought the Count over here it was just to meet you," she said. "But I saw his eyes light up when he heard who you were. Did he make an offer?"

"He mentioned something," Clint said.

"I'll bet," Emmy said, "he wants to make you his headliner."

"He did mention that."

"That's not gonna make Johnny Sharp very happy," she said.

"And who's Johnny Sharp?"

"Right now he's our sharp shooter," she said, "and our headliner."

"Thanks for telling me that," Clint said. "I'm not here to step on any toes."

"I know," she said, "you're here for a meal and a bed. Why don't I show you where you can bed down?"

Clint stood, picked up his rifle and saddlebags and said, "Let's go."

***

Emmy lead Clint through Freakville.

"None of these people," he said, looking around at the collection of oddities moving about, "mind the town's name?"

"I told you," she said. "We all know we're freaks, so no. To us the name makes sense."

"And it was the Count who named it?"

"Yes."

"And does anybody know *his* real name?" Clint asked. "Or is he just 'the Count' to everyone?"

"Right now he's giving us all a place to sleep and eat," Emmy said, "so nobody really cares what his real name is."

They stopped in front of one of the few buildings in town that still had all four of its walls.

"What happened to this town?" he asked. "And what was it called before?"

"The answer to those questions is easy," she said. "I don't know."

They entered what looked to have one time been a hotel. Where there normally would have been a front desk there was only an empty space.

"There are always rooms available, here," she told Clint, pointing up the stairs. "I can't get my fat ass up those steps, so you go on up and grab a room."

"How do I know which ones are available?" he asked.

"The empty rooms are the ones with the doors open," she said. "Get yourself settled. Come on back to the mess tent when you're ready and I'll introduce you to some more of our people."

"I'll be there," Clint said.

He was fascinated by the population of Freakville and was looking forward to meeting more of the citizens. He also had the Count's offer to consider, but there was really no serious possibility of him accepting, especially when he heard about Johnny Sharp. He wasn't looking to take anybody's job away from them.

He had barely chosen his room and closed the door when there was a knock. He set his rifle and saddlebags down on the bed and went to the door, his hand near his gun.

"Who is it?"

"It's me," a voice said. "Bizzy."

When Clint opened the door, the little red-haired man glared up at him.

"What's on your mind, Bizzy?" Clint asked.

"I heard who you are," Bizzy said, "and I ain't impressed."

"I'm not asking you to be impressed," Clint said.

"Yeah, well Emmy's impressed," Bizzy said. "And she's my wife. I don't want you gettin' no ideas about her."

Clint couldn't believe the little man was serious, but he also didn't want to insult him.

"Look, Bizzy," Clint said, "she's a lovely woman, but I don't make it a habit to get between husbands and wives, so you have nothing to worry about."

"You better keep it that way," Bizzy said, emphasizing his words by pointing his finger again and again. "You got it?"

"I've got it."

Bizzy stuck out his jaw, nodded his head, turned and stormed off down the hall.

Clint closed the door, shaking his head, thinking he had never seen a couple odder than Bizzy and Emmy. He couldn't even imagine how they had consummated their union.

He went to the bed and sat down. The room was still set up like any hotel room. He looked around—in drawers, the closet—to see if there was anything to indicate what the hotel, or the town, had been called. He didn't find a thing, so he went to the pitcher-and-basin on the dresser. The pitcher was filled with water, and he proceeded to clean up.

Chapter Five

The Count had set up an office for himself in what used to be City Hall. His assistant was another little man, Bobo, who stood just an inch under four feet tall. He had sent Bobo out to find Johnny Sharp.

"That's all, Bobo," the Count said.

"Right, boss."

"What's on your mind, Count?"

The Count looked at the young man seated across from him. He was tall, slender, handsome, under thirty, and very accurate with a pistol or a rifle. Just the kind of man he needed as a headliner, until . . .

"I don't know if you heard," the Count said, "but Bizzy and Emmy brought a stranger in today."

"I heard. You meet 'im?"

"I did," the Count said. "It's Clint Adams."

Sharp's eyes got wide.

"The Gunsmith?"

"That's right."

"What's he doin' here?"

"Passing through, as far as I know," the Count said. "Emmy took him to the old hotel to get a room."

"How long's he gonna be stayin'?"

"I don't know, Johnny," the Count said. "But I was thinking he'd make a helluva headliner."

"Wait a minute," Sharp said. "You tol' me I was gonna be your headliner for your new show."

"I know I told you that, Johnny, but . . . well, he *is* the Gunsmith."

"Did you offer him the job?"

"Not really," the Count said. "I mentioned it to him."

"Did he say he wants it?"

"No, he didn't make a decision."

Sharp sat forward in his chair.

"So you did offer it to him."

"I just mentioned the possibility," the Count said. "Nothing's been decided."

"Yeah, it has!" Sharp said, jumping to his feet. "You been tellin' me I was the headliner."

"Johnny, be reasonable—"

"I'll show you," Sharp said. "Make him shoot against me. I'll show you *and* him who's the best."

"Wait a minute," the Count said.

"What?"

"That's a great idea, Johnny," the Count said. "That'd be a great headlining act."

"Whataya talkin' about?"

"You against the Gunsmith," the Count said. "Look, just leave it to me and you'll still be the headliner."

"I just want you to keep your word, Count," Sharp said.

"Like I said," the Count replied, "leave it to me."

Sharp turned and stormed out.

***

The Count had not only taken over City Hall, but he lived in the old mayor's house, on the south end of town.

"Belle," he called out, as he entered, "are you here?"

Belle St. Clair came into the room, her gardenia perfume preceding her. She had acres of black hair that cascaded down over her shoulders, luminous blue eyes, and full, luscious lips. There was also a bored expression on her face that the Count was constantly fighting to remove.

"Where else would I be?" she asked. "There's nothing to do around here."

"Well," he said, "I may have found something to occupy your time."

"Is that right?" She was wearing a purple robe that extended all the way to the floor but clung to the curves of her voluptuous form. "And what would that be?"

"I need you to beguile a man."

"Oh, that," she said. "What man did you have in mind, darling?"

"His name is Clint Adams."

She frowned.

"I know that name, don't I?"

"He's also known as The Gunsmith."

"Well, well," she said, "now it gets interesting. What do we want from him?"

"He's here and we want him to stay here," the Count said.

"Ah," she said, "as your new headliner? How does Johnny Sharp feel about that?"

"Don't you worry about Johnny," he said. "Do you still have him wrapped around your little finger?"

"Oh, yes," she said. "Nice and tight."

"Then I need you to do the same thing to the Gunsmith," the Count said.

"Do you want him to fall in love with me?" she asked.

"I want him to choose to stay with us," the Count said. "I don't care how you do it."

"And tell me, darling," she said, "do you care if I enjoy my work?"

Chapter Six

Belle found Emmy in the mess tent, eating again. She sat down across the table from her.

"Whatayou want?" Emmy asked, wiping her mouth.

"I heard you brought in a stranger earlier today," Belle said.

"That's right."

"I want to meet him."

"He won't like you," Emmy said.

"Why do you say that?"

"He likes someone who's . . . more woman."

Belle smiled, trying not to laugh. "You mean, like you?"

"How do you know that?" Belle asked.

"I see the way he looks at me," Emmy said, around a mouthful of stew.

"Is that right?"

"And," Emmy said, "he put his hand on my butt."

"My, my," Belle said, "now I know I have to meet this mysterious man."

"Well, go ahead," Emmy said. "Meet 'im."

"The Count wants you to introduce me," Belle told her.

Emmy put her spoon down and sat back, glaring at the beautiful woman.

"Did he say that?"

"He did," Belle said. "He told me that just half-an-hour ago. You can check with him, if you don't believe me."

"I don't like this," Emmy said. "Are you gonna make him fall in love with you?"

"Now how would I do that?"

"You're a witch, ain'tcha?"

"My dear," Belle said, "you know that I'm a white witch. We don't do evil magic."

"That depends on what you think evil magic is," Emmy said.

"Will you introduce us, or shall I tell the Count—" Belle started.

"Oh, I'll introduce you," Emmy said, cutting her off. "He'll be down here soon, and I think you'll see that he's immune to your charms."

"Really?" Belle said. "That will be interesting, as I don't think I've ever met a man who is immune to me."

"Well, Clint's gonna be one," Emmy said, "and my husband, Bizzy, is another."

"Oh yes," Belle said, "your little husband. I believe if I was the least bit interested in little men, I could have him in a minute."

"You're welcome to try," Emmy said.

Belle was about to retort but thought better of it. Since Bizzy had married the hefty Emmy, maybe he *would* be immune to Belle's charms. He obviously liked large women.

"That's all right," she said. "You can keep your husband."

"Do me a favor, Belle," Emmy said. "Go sit somewhere else. I'll bring Clint Adams over to you when he gets here. You're ruinin' my meal."

Belle just smiled, stood up and moved to another table.

***

Clint finished washing up, put on a fresh shirt, then decided to clean his guns before doing anything else. After all, he had been on the trail for a while, and that meant lots of dirt and dust.

When he knew the weapons were in proper working order he set the rifle aside, strapped on his gunbelt and slid the Colt into the holster. He didn't think he would have a need for the guns, but it never hurt to keep them clean.

He left his room and walked down the hall, passing a person who appeared to be half-man, half-woman. Both halves smiled at him, so he nodded back. So far, this was the only citizen of Freakville who had unnerved him, slightly. He couldn't imagine what his/her name might be.

On the street he passed a few more of Freakville's population. Some nodded to him, some ignored him. Some of them seemed very normal. Having spent time with P.T. Barnum and Buffalo Bill Cody, he knew that any kind of show had to have workers behind the scenes. He assumed the normal men he saw were those workers.

He made his way to the mess tent, as promised, and saw Emmy sitting at a table alone. It was probably her size that kept people from sitting with her, because her personality was about as sunny as could be. He walked over and joined her.

"There you are," she said, happily. "Do you wanna eat again?"

"Not til later," he said. "I had enough earlier."

She looked down at her heaping plate, then at him and said, "My problem is, I can never have enough."

"Don't let me stop you," Clint said.

"There's someone here who wants to meet you," she said. "I'll just finish this plate and then make the intro-duction."

"No problem," he said, "I'll wait."

And while he waited, he looked over at the beautiful, black-haired woman who was sitting alone.

Chapter Seven

"Who's this person who wanted to meet me?" Clint asked Emmy.

"You're lookin' at her," Emmy said.

"The black-haired woman? She's beautiful."

"And she knows it," Emmy said. "She's gonna try and make you fall in love with her."

"Why?"

"Because that's what she does," Emmy said. Then she lowered her voice. "She's a witch."

"A witch?"

Emmy nodded.

"A white witch."

"I didn't know witches came in different colors," he said. "What's the difference?"

"White witches are supposed to be good," Emmy said.

"But you don't believe that?"

"I don't think you can trust any witch," Emmy said.

"Then why are you going to introduce me?"

"She told me the Count wants me to introduce you to her."

"Ah," Clint said, "I get it, now."

"Get what?"

"The Count wants that woman to get me to stay."

"Stay for what?"

"To be his headliner."

"Oh, that," Emmy said. "Johnny's not gonna like that."

"Johnny . . . Sharp?" Clint said. "Is that his real name? Or a stage name."

"You know about stage names?"

"Sure," Clint said. "I spent some time with P.T. Barnum and Buffalo Bill Cody."

"You knew P.T. Barnum?"

"I met him," Clint said. "Spent time with him in New York."

"New York City?"

"Yes," he said, "Manhattan."

Her eyes got wide.

"That must've been excitin'."

"Maybe the Count will take his show to New York," Clint said.

"With you as a headliner, he probably would," she said. "Oh, she's lookin' over here. I better introduce you now."

"Let's do it," Clint said.

They both stood up and walked over to the other table. As they reached it the woman smiled. She was breathtakingly beautiful. Clint could see how she got men to fall in love with her.

"Belle St. Clair," Emmy said, "meet Clint Adams."

"Mr. Adams," Belle said. "Won't you sit with me?"

She had the bluest eyes he'd ever seen. If he didn't know better, he might have fallen in love with her right there and then.

"Thank you, Emmy," Belle said. "You can go, now."

Emmy looked at Clint as he sat across from Belle, and hoped she was right about him. She walked away.

"Sorry about that," Belle said. "I don't like being around her."

"Why not?" Clint asked. "She's a very sweet person."

"Yes, she is," Belle said, "but look at her. Do you know what she weighs?"

"Three hundred?" he guessed.

"Three sixty," Belle said. "Can you imagine?"

"She seems to move pretty well for a woman her size," Clint said.

"So you like her?"

"I do," Clint said, "very much."

"You better look out for her husband. He's a vicious little thing."

"Bizzy and I have already had words," Clint said. "We understand each other."

"If you understand Bizzy, then you're in the minority," she said.

"So tell me," Clint said, "why does the Count want us to meet?"

Belle frowned.

"Emmy told you that?"

"She did."

"Did she also tell you I'm a witch?"

"A white witch," Clint said. "I didn't know what that was, so she explained it to me."

"Emmy has no idea what it means to be a white witch," Belle said.

"Then why don't you tell me what it is?"

"A white witch practices magic for the greater good of everyone," Belle said. "There is no evil in what I do."

"So you make men fall in love with you for their own good?" he asked.

"If men fall in love with me," she said, "it's not because of anything I do. For instance, I'm just sitting here. Are you in love with me?"

"No," he said, "but let's give it some time and see what happens."

Chapter Eight

"Why don't we go for a walk," she said, standing, "and get to know one another."

They left the tent and started strolling. The dress she wore looked as if it had been made specifically for her body. It was purple and fit like a second skin.

"What are you doing here, Belle?" he asked. "A woman as smart and beautiful as you can probably do anything."

"You'd think so, wouldn't you," she said. "But men only want me to do one thing."

"And you won't do it?"

"I will," she said, "but under my own rules."

"So tell me," Clint said, "do you have an act?"

"I do," she said.

"And how did the Count find you?"

"Oh, we know each other for a long time," she said. "We've been in a couple of shows together. So when he decided he was going to have his own, he contacted me and asked me to come here."

"And you came," Clint said. "What did you think when you got here and saw the name of the town?"

"Why not?" she asked. "We're all freaks—even you."

"I'm a freak?" he asked.

"Aren't you a freak of nature with your gun?" she asked.

"I suppose I never looked at it that way," he said, "but you may be right."

"Do you ever miss?"

"No."

"There you are," she said. "You can't be perfect and not be a freak."

Clint noticed that the people they were passing were ignoring them, rather than greeting them.

"Why do I get the feeling nobody in this town likes you?" he asked.

"I can only assume they're all afraid of me," she said.

"But you're a white witch," he said. "Don't they know that?"

"To most people," she said, "a witch is a witch. There's no difference."

"I think everyone here is unique in their own way," Clint said. "At least, from what I've seen. Why would they hold anything against you?"

"Well," she said, "I also have a special relationship with the Count. I think they're jealous of that."

"Special?"

"Yes," she said, "we've been friends a long time."

"Then you know his real name."

"Of course."

"And can you say what it is?"

"No," she said, "that's up to him."

Clint suddenly realized they were on a deserted street, which she had steered them to.

"Where are we going?" he asked.

"Like I said," she answered, "just walking and getting to know each other."

"Can I ask you some questions?"

"Of course."

"When do you think the Count will have his show ready?"

"I can't say that, either," she said, "but we're all ready."

"Will he be using everyone in town?"

"Probably not," she said. "Only the best."

"Like Johnny Sharp?"

"Ah," she said, "Johnny. Another freak with a gun. I've never seen Johnny miss. That's why the Count was going to make him the headliner."

"Was?"

"Well," she said, "you're here, now."

"I'm not here to take anybody's job," Clint said.

Freakville

"If Johnny's good enough," she said, "he'll keep his spot."

"I think maybe I should meet him."

"I think you should meet a lot of the people here," she said. "But to do that, you'll have to stay a while."

"That's not a problem," he said. "I wasn't going any-where in particular when I saw the Freakville sign. I'm curious enough to stick around a while. If that's what the Count wanted you to get me to say, you can tell him you did it."

"This is my place," she said, as they stopped in front of a small house.

"Are you inviting me in?" he asked.

"Of course not," she said. "We've only just met. The Count didn't send me to sleep with you, he sent me to get to know you."

"And did you do that?"

"Not completely," she said, "but it's a start. Can you find your way back to your room?"

"I think so."

"Then maybe I'll see you tomorrow," she said. "Thanks for walking me home."

He watched as she went up the walk, unlocked the door and went inside. Then he turned and left.

***

35

Belle watched from the window to make sure Clint Adams had left the area. Then she headed for the Count's house.

Chapter Nine

Clint didn't go back to his room, but to the mess tent, hoping to find Emmy there. He needn't have worried. She was still sitting there, eating. Around her was a whole new group of what Clint preferred to think of as oddities, rather than freaks.

He walked to Emmy's table, she seemed surprised to see him. Or perhaps it was relief.

"She didn't get you," she said. "I knew she wouldn't."

"Get me?"

"You know the Count sent her to bewitch you," Emmy said.

"Well," Clint said, "then she didn't do a very good job."

"What did the two of you do?"

"We just walked," Clint said. "We ended up in front of her house, and she went in."

"Her house?"

"Yes," he said, "a small, wooden—"

"Those houses are empty," she said, cutting him off.

"If she doesn't live there, where does she live?" he asked.

"She lives with the Count, in his house," Emmy said.

"She told me they were friends," Clint said. "Are they more than that?"

"Nobody knows what goes on in that house," Emmy said. "A lot of people think they're lovers, but nobody knows for sure."

"And how often does he use her like this?" he asked. "To interest a man in staying?"

"Not just men," Emmy said.

"That's interesting."

"I'll tell you the truth," she said, "because nobody else will."

"I'm listening."

"I want you to stay," she said. "Johnny Sharp's gonna want you to go, and so are others, because you're not one of us. So the decision's gonna be yours but watch out for Belle."

"And the Count?" Clint asked. "He's the one who sent Belle after me."

"He'll use whatever he can to put his show together. He's determined."

"So there's good and bad in the Count."

"I see the good more than the bad," she said. "It's just . . . the witch. She may have even used her powers on him."

That made sense to Clint.

At that moment Bizzy came strutting into the tent and headed straight for them.

"I thought I'd find you here with him!" he snapped.

"I'm eatin'," she said.

"You're always eatin'!" he said, "We got work to do." He gave Clint a hard look.

"I was just talking to Emmy about Belle St. Clair," Clint said. "What's your take on her, Bizzy?"

"That bitch is a witch, pure and simple. She can't be trusted."

"How do you feel about the Count?"

"If he gets this show put together, I'll feel fine about 'im. If he don't, then he'll be just another poser to me." The little man looked at Emmy. "Let's go!"

"Yes, dear," she said, standing. They presented a very odd sight as they left the tent together, side-by-side.

"It's hard to believe, ain't it?"

Clint turned and saw Smilin' Jack.

"What's hard to believe, exactly?" Clint asked.

"Those two sharin' a bed," Jack said, shaking his head. "That's somethin' I'd like to see."

"Actually," Clint said, "that's something I don't want to see."

"I get it," Jack said. "Listen, I came lookin' for you because some of us have a poker game going a few nights a week, and tonight's one of those nights. I thought you might like to join us."

"Poker," Clint said. "What stakes?"

"Nothin' big," Jack said. "It's just somethin' to occupy us while we're waitin' for the Count to get his show together."

"Where do you play?"

"We set up a table in the big top tent," Jack said. "If you like, you can find us there tonight after nine o'clock. The tent is used for other things, but at night it's empty— except for us."

"And you have room for me?"

"We usually play with five," Jack said. "Six won't be a problem."

"Well, then," Clint said, "I may just stop by."

"Great!" the rubber-faced man said. "See you tonight." He started away, then stopped. "Oh, we'll also have some drinks available."

"Sounds good."

Jack turned and left the tent.

Clint knew there were several towns nearby—one he passed on the way, and a few others in the area. Freakville probably got its supplies from a mercantile in one of those towns.

Clint thought a poker game would be a good way to get to know some of the other oddities in town.

Chapter Ten

Clint walked into the big top tent at nine-oh-five. The wagon Bizzy had driven in was off to one side. In the center was a round table with five people seated at it.

"You made it," Jack said, standing up. "Let me introduce you around the table."

Clint looked at the collection of oddities he was going to play poker with.

"That's Raza, he's a knife thrower." Raza was dark-skinned, could have been Mexican, but he was wearing a turban, so he was probably from India. The man nodded.

"That's Gordo, he's our strong man." Gordo was big, black man.

"That fella right there, he's Destro the Great."

"What's great about him?" Clint asked.

Destro smiled, waved his hand and four aces appeared.

"He's a magician," Jack said, "but don't worry, he doesn't use his magic in the game."

"I hope not," Clint said.

"And finally, that's Lefty. He's a juggler. And if you look close, you'll see he has six fingers on his left hand."

Clint did look close, and he could see a second little finger.

"How does that help when you deal?" Clint asked him.

"You'll find out," Lefty said, with a grin.

"Have a seat," Jack said. He, Lefty and Destro were smiling. Both Raza and the strong man, Gordo, were very somber.

Clint sat in the empty chair and Jack said, "How about a whiskey?"

"One shot," Clint said. "I don't usually drink when I'm playing cards."

"That'll give you an advantage," Destro said, "because we all do."

"You play drunk?" Clint asked.

"Not Gordo," Destro said. "He's got two hollow legs."

Jack brought a shot glass of whiskey to the table for Clint and sat down.

"Where are all you fellas from?" Clint asked.

Jack answered for everyone.

"Raza is from India, Gordo's Jamaican, Lefty's from Ireland, while Destro is from Italy. Me, I came west from New York City."

"I've spent time in New York," Clint said. "That's where I met P.T. Barnum. But I've never been to any of your homes."

"You would love Ireland," Lefty said. "It's a beautiful country."

"You don't have an Irish accent," Clint said.

"I used to, when I first came here," Lefty said, "but I learned real quick that Americans didn't like Irishmen, so I trained myself to speak without my accent."

"And Destro, you don't have an Italian accent."

"Like Lefty, I trained it out of myself," Destro said. "I didn't experience the hatred Lefty did, but I thought it was a good idea."

"Sometimes," Jack said, "in his act, he puts it on again."

"Well," Destro said, "it does help with the magic."

"Why don't we play cards?" Jack said. "Clint, new guy deals."

Clint put his money on the table, picked up the cards and said, "Five card draw."

***

The stakes started low but got higher. Pennies became nickels, nickels became dimes, and dimes became two bits.

"A dollar," said six-fingered Lefty.

"As soon as you get lucky you wanna raise the stakes," Jack said.

"How else can I get my money back," Lefty asked. "I open for a dollar."

They were playing another hand of five card draw, which was Clint's preferred game. He found that stud games took too long.

"Okay," Jack said, "I'm in." He tossed a dollar into the pot.

"Call," Gordo said. The strong man had only said a few words over the past hour, like "call" or "fold," or the number of cards he wanted to draw. When he opened, he just tossed the money in.

"Allah says I should call," Raza said and tossed in his dollar. He smiled at Lefty. "He tells me you are bluffing."

"Then why don't you raise?" Lefty asked.

"Allah has not told me to raise," Raza said.

"Maybe you should make some decisions on your own, instead of waitin' for Allah to tell you," Lefty said.

"Never mind," Clint said, as the bet came around to him. "I'll raise a dollar."

"You think I'm bluffin', too?" Lefty asked.

"No," Clint said. Indeed, he didn't care whether Lefty was bluffing or not. Destro, the magician, had dealt him a full house, three nines and two tens.

"I fold," Destro said. "Back to you, Lefty. Clint raised you."

"I'm payin' attention, Destro!" Lefty snapped. He stared across the table at Clint. "Okay, I call and raise you two dollars."

Jack folded, Gordo called, and Raza folded. That made it two dollars to Clint, who wondered what Gordo was still doing in the hand.

The three players who had folded must have had horrible hands they didn't think they could improve, to fold even before they drew cards.

Destro said to Lefty, "How many?"

"I'll play these," Lefty said.

"Mr. Adams?"

"I told you, it's just Clint."

"Okay," Destro said, "how many, Clint?"

"None," Clint said. "I'm good."

Now they all looked at the strong man.

"Three," Gordo said.

Destro dealt him the cards.

"Up to you, Lefty."

"Let's play like men," Lefty said. "Five dollars."

That drew some looks from the players who had dropped out.

Clint had been in high stakes games where hundreds, even thousands of dollars were on the table. Five dollars was a big bet in this game.

"Are you sure?" Destro asked.

"I'm sure," Lefty said.

He had a full house, or four of a kind. Either way, Clint's full house was not a lock. And then there was Gordo. He had drawn three or a pair. It remained to be seen if he was going to stay in.

"Clint?" Destro said.

Clint studied Lefty across the table, then looked at Gordo. The big black strong man was staring at his cards. Lefty was tapping that sixth finger of his.

He was bluffing.

"I call," Clint said, "and raise five."

"Gordo," Destro said, "ten dollars to you."

The strong man finally looked up from his cards, glanced at Clint and Lefty, then said, "I call," and tossed in the money.

Clint wondered if his full house could come in third.

Chapter Eleven

Gordo called, even knowing that Lefty might raise, again.

Lefty looked across the table at Clint, his sixth finger tapping away. Then it stopped.

"I call," he said.

Clint showed his hand.

"Full house, nines over tens," Destro said. "Lefty?"

Lefty didn't show his hand. He just threw it on the table, face down.

"Gordo?" Destro said.

"What?" the strong man asked.

"Show your cards," Destro said. "Clint has a full house. Can you beat it?"

Gordo put his cards down, face up. He had nothing, not even a pair.

"Oh my God," Lefty said, "at least when I was bluffing, I had *some*thing."

"I have nothing?" Gordo asked.

"No, Gord," Destro said, "you don't."

Gordo just shrugged.

It had become clear to Clint early that Gordo didn't know the rules of the game, although in this hand he might have caught on and actually had something.

Lefty's tell of tapping his sixth finger when he had nothing came in handy the rest of the night. Of the other players, Raza also had a tell. He became very quiet when he had a good hand and talked when he had a bad one. As for Jack, there was no tell, but he was a terrible poker player.

Destro was the only player with no tell, and who seemed to know the game. Given the fact that he was a magician, he probably could have won every hand, but it seemed to Clint that the magic man was playing a clean game.

Gordo continued to lose and didn't seem to mind. He stayed in every hand, no matter what he had. Lefty continued to try to bluff and became more and more agitated. Jack's smile never left his rubber face, whether he won a hand, or lost it.

Clint won steadily and might have felt guilty about it if the stakes were higher. There were no more five-dollar bets after that particular hand, but there were also no two bit bets. They seemed to have settled on a dollar or two.

The game went on past midnight. If it was meant to be a social thing, the five men didn't talk much. Which suited Clint, though, since he liked playing at a quiet table, with no one boasting or bellyaching.

The other five men also kept drinking whiskey, but all seemed to have a tolerance for it. Their drunkeness was nothing sloppy or nasty, except that eventually, Lefty got tired of losing.

"That's it for me, gents," he said, standing just after midnight. "My luck can't be that bad, so I think Destro's up to his tricks."

"I don't know all of you very well," Clint said, "but I know poker, and I can tell you Destro has been dealing a clean game."

"Then how can I be losin' so steadily?" Lefty demanded.

"I could tell you," Clint said, "but it's not something you usually give away."

Lefty's eyes narrowed.

"You noticed somethin' about my play?" he asked.

"Most players have a tell," Clint said. "I can say that much."

"What's mine?"

"It wouldn't be fair to the others if I told you," Clint said.

"Do we all have tells?" Jack asked Clint.

"Not all," Clint said. "I can tell you that Gordo and Jack, you don't. Neither does Destro.

Lefty sat back down.

"This is interestin'," he said. "You're sayin' me and Raza have tells, Jack and Destro don't. What about Gordo?"

"If I'm right," Clint said, "Gordo just likes to play, and doesn't care if he wins or loses."

They all looked at the strong man, who nodded.

"Why am I losin'?" Jack asked.

"Jack, you're just not a very good player."

"I can accept that," Jack said.

"And I'm bad?" Lefty asked.

"You'd do better if you didn't try to bluff so often and give it away."

Lefty looked around the table.

"We're all friends here. Nobody's lookin' to take everybody's money. Does anybody mind if Clint clues us in? Raza?"

"I would like to know how I am giving away my hands," Raza admitted.

"Destro?" Lefty asked.

"Doesn't matter to me," Destro said. "Like Lefty says, it should be interesting."

"All right," Clint said. "It's your sixth finger, Lefty."

Lefty looked down at his hand.

"What about it?"

"When you bluff, that sixth finger taps your cards."

Lefty looked at his hand again.

"I never noticed," he commented. "So you knew every time I was bluffin'?"

"Yes," Clint said, "and you bluff too often."

"And me?" Raza asked.

"When you have a good hand, you're very quiet," Clint said. "But when you have a bad hand, or you're bluffing, you talk very quickly and a lot."

"By Allah," Raza hissed, "I never knew that."

"Looks like we all learned something tonight," Destro said. He flicked his wrist and was suddenly holding four Queens. "Maybe I *should* start using my magic in poker games."

"If you had *real* magic," Clint said, "that would be a bad idea."

"You don't believe in magic?" Destro asked.

"No," Clint said. "If I did, and you used it in a poker game, I might have to use my gun."

"You could only use your gun," Destro said, "if it was loaded."

"I always keep my gun loaded."

"Do you?" Destro asked. He put his left fist on the table, then opened it. In his hand were five bullets.

Chapter Twelve

Once he revealed why he was winning so much the game was over. All the players left, except for Destro and Jack, who invited Clint to stay for more drinks. Since they weren't playing anymore, he agreed. The three of them sat at the poker table with a bottle of whiskey.

"I'm assuming by now you met Belle St. Clair," Destro said.

"What makes you say that?" Clint asked.

"She's the Count's secret weapon," Destro said. "We all know he's going to try to sign you up."

"Johnny's not gonna like it," Jack said.

"I've got to meet this Johnny Sharp," Clint said.

"Oh, you will," Destro said. "Johnny's very confident. He's not going to back down from shooting against you."

"He's also not going to like that the Count sent Belle after you."

"Don't tell me," Clint said. "He's in love with her."

"We're all in love with her," Destro said. "We don't have much choice. Hasn't she put her spell on you, yet?"

"No," Clint said, "apparently not. You, Jack?"

"Oh yeah," the rubber-faced man said, with his smile. "None of the men here can help it."

"What about Bizzy?" Clint asked.

"That's different," Destro said. "Bizzy's got Emmy."

"What about the other women here?" Clint asked.

"Some of them are in love with Belle, too," Destro said.

"Aren't there other couples here?" Clint asked.

"There's Tina and Carlos," Destro said. "They're aerialists, and they're married, so Belle hasn't cast her spell on them."

"Anyone else?"

Destro and Jack exchanged a glance.

"What is it?" Clint asked.

"We're both thinking of Kyra," Destro said.

"And who is Kyra?"

"She's also a witch," Jack said, "but not a white one."

"Ah," Clint said, "so she's an evil witch?"

"She doesn't claim a title," Destro said. "Not white, not black, not evil or good. She's just . . . a witch."

"She and Belle don't get along," Destro said.

"Well," Clint said, "now I'm looking forward to meeting Kyra."

"We can arrange that tomorrow," Jack said. "Another drink?"

"Why not?" Clint asked. "What else is there to do?"

Chapter Thirteen

Clint woke the next morning with a sour mouth from too much whiskey the night before. Whiskey was not his drink of choice, but he had enjoyed sharing a bottle with Jack and Destro. They had gotten to the point where Destro started to do magic tricks with a deck of cards. But what impressed Clint was when he got back to his room and finally checked his gun, he found it unloaded, except for one round under the chamber. Destro knew who he was dealing with and did not leave Clint defenseless. But how he got those bullets out of his gun, Clint had no idea. If he didn't know better, he'd believe it was magic. But he preferred to think that it had been some sort of sleight of hand trick. Still, even that was impressive.

Jack didn't do any tricks, but he did show Clint just how rubber he was by bending his fingers back at one point. Clint was surprised they didn't snap.

He dressed and strapped on his gun, which he had reloaded before going to bed. As he entered the mess tent, he saw a line of people waiting for their breakfast. There was a smaller line at the coffee pot, so he went there first.

When he had his coffee, he walked to a table where three people he had never met were seated.

"Mind if I join you?" he asked.

The young man seated across from the pretty young woman said, "Please, do join us," in slightly accented English.

He sat next to the man, who turned to him and said, "I am Carlos, and this is Tina, my wife."

"Ah," Clint said, "you're the aerialists."

"Yes, we are," Tina said. "How did you know?"

"I played poker with some folks last night," Clint said. "They mentioned you."

Carlos was a strapping young man, and Tina was a wisp of a girl. The difference between them was not as great as the difference between Bizzy and Emmy, but it was noticeable.

The third person at the table looked at Clint and nodded.

"This is Electro," Carlos said. "Do not attempt to shake his hand. He is electrically charged."

"Really?" Clint said. "Wow, that's interesting."

Looking at their plates, Clint realized they were all eating steak-and-eggs.

"Won't you be eating?" Tina asked. She didn't have her husband's accent but sounded completely American.

"The line's kind of long—" he said.

"No, no," she said, "you're our guest." She stood up. "I'll get you a plate."

"Wait," he said, "yours'll get cold—" But she was gone, running to the front of the line to get him a plate of food.

"Don't worry," Carlos said. "Nobody says no to Tina. She'll be right back."

True to Carlos' words, Tina came hurrying back with a plate and set it in front of Clint. He had steak-and-eggs and a couple of buttered biscuits.

"It looks great," he said, as she sat back down. "Thank you."

"I figured you'd like those biscuits buttered," she said. "That's the way Carlos likes them."

"You figured right," he said, and started to eat.

"Where do you folks get your supplies?" he asked.

"We are fifty miles from Flagstaff," Carlos said. "Twice a month the Count chooses two of us to take a wagon there and stock up."

"Where are you from, Carlos?" Clint asked. "I can't place your accent. It's not Mexican."

"No, sir," Carlos said, "I am from Brazil."

"I've been to South America, but it was years ago," Clint said. "How long have you been in this country?"

"I came here with my parents when I was ten," he said. "They died when I was fifteen. I was in an orphanage for a little while, and then I met Tina."

The couple looked to still be in their twenties.

He looked at the other oddities seated at tables around him, saw Jack, and Destro and the strong man, Gordo. He didn't see the Count, or Belle.

"Does the Count usually eat here, as well?" he asked.

"He never eats with us," Carlos said. "He takes his meals at his house."

"And Belle?"

"She eats with him," Tina said. Clint noticed the harshness of the word "she" as it came out of her mouth.

"There's someone else I've been told I should meet," Clint said.

"Who is that?" Carlos asked.

"Kyra."

Carlos, Tina and Electro stopped eating and stared at Clint.

"Does she take her meals here?" he asked.

"Kyra does what she wants," Tina said, "where she wants."

"There are no restaurants in town, are there?" he asked.

"No," Carlos said, as he, his wife and Electro began eating again, "this is the only place to get food. But some eat it here, and some . . . elsewhere."

Like the Count? And Kyra?"

"And Belle," Tina said.

"If Belle and Kyra don't get along," Clint asked, "do they have any friends?"

"Belle has the Count," Carlos said. "Kyra doesn't seem to have any friends."

"She doesn't want any," Tina said, sounding bitter. Clint looked at her and she added, "I tried."

"Tina's very friendly," Carlos said. "Kyra is not."

Clint smiled.

"I find it hard to believe anyone wouldn't want to be Tina's friend."

"Thank you, Mr. Adams," Tina said.

He hadn't told them his name, so it was clear the word had gotten around.

"Just call me Clint."

Chapter Fourteen

As he finished his breakfast Clint thought it might be time to meet Johnny Sharp.

"Does Johnny eat in here?" he asked.

"Usually," Carlos said. "He should probably be along shortly."

"He's not happy about you being here," Tina said. "He's going to want to prove himself."

"Well, I hope that means targets," Clint said.

"Oh yes," Tina said, "Johnny's not a killer. He's just a very talented sharpshooter."

Clint wondered if Tina's husband noticed the reverence she seemed to exhibit when she talked about Johnny Sharp?

"Everybody's a killer," Electro said.

"What?" Carlos said.

"Under the right circumstance," the man said, "everybody can be a killer." He snapped his fingers and a spark appeared. "It can happen just like that."

"You seem to be speaking from experience," Clint said.

"I've seen my share of killers," he said.

The man looked to be in his forties, so that was probably true.

"Well, not Johnny," Tina said.

Clint saw Carlos peering at his wife over his coffee cup.

"I guess I'll get another cup of coffee and wait for him to arrive," Clint said. "Excuse me. I should say good-morning to Emmy, also."

Emmy had entered while they were talking, stood in line, got her breakfast and grabbed a table. Clint filled his coffee cup and walked to her table.

"Do you mind?" he asked.

"I don't," she said, "but Bizzy might."

"Would you prefer I don't sit?"

"No, no," she said, "please, sit down. If Bizzy doesn't like it, too bad."

He sat across from her. She was wearing a billowy brown dress, but unlike yesterday, this one covered her all the way to her neck.

"Is Bizzy the reason nobody ever sits with you?" Clint asked.

"Either that, or nobody wants to sit with the fat lady," she said. "Take your pick."

"You know," he said, "I would think you'd have lots of friends. I mean, with your personality."

"That's nice of you to say."

"What about Tina?" Clint asked. "She seems friendly enough."

"Tina's a sweet girl," she said, "but she has to sit with her husband."

"She *has* to?"

"Carlos is real controlling," she said.

"Can I ask you something?" he said.

"Anything." She chewed and listened.

"I notice something in Tina's voice when she talks about Johnny Sharp."

"You're observant," she said. "Yes, I believe Tina has a big crush on Johnny."

"Does her husband have any idea?"

"I'd think so," she said, "but as far as I know, they've never talked about it. At least, not in public."

"And how does Johnny feel about her?"

"Like most of the men here," she said, "Johnny's in love with Belle."

"Are we talking about lust," he asked, "or real love?"

"When men see her, it starts as lust," she said, "but then it becomes love. They have no choice."

"Because she's a witch?"

"Exactly" Emmy said, then she peered at him with interest. "Have you fallen in love with her yet?"

"I haven't."

"Give it time."

Chapter Fifteen

While Clint sat there and watched Emmy eat enough food to sustain three men, Bizzy entered the tent. He saw them together and came straight to their table.

"Why am I always findin' you with him?" Bizzy demanded.

"The Count told me to introduce him around," Emmy said. "You want me to do what the Count says, right?"

She had him there.

"I guess so." He glared at Clint.

"I'm waiting to meet Johnny Sharp," Clint told him.

"Get some breakfast and join us, hon," Emmy said.

"Yeah," Bizzy said, "yeah, I think I will."

"I'll get you some coffee," Emmy told her husband. "Wait here."

"Sure."

She grabbed his cup, too, and went over to the coffee. She came back with full cups for Clint and Bizzy, then went back to eating. When Bizzy returned, he was carrying more plates than Clint would have thought possible for the little man.

"I thought Lefty was the juggler," Clint kidded.

"Bizzy's got lots of talents, don't you, hon?" Emmy asked.

"I got enough."

"I'll bet the Count, uh, counts on you, huh?" Clint asked.

Bizzy scowled at him, then started eating.

Watching this husband-and-wife eat was an experience. Bizzy managed to eat at least as much as Emmy did, which was amazing, considering his size.

They were still eating when a young man wearing a gun on his hip, and a wide, white Stetson, entered the tent and went to get some breakfast.

"There's your boy," Bizzy said.

"Johnny?" Clint asked.

Bizzy nodded.

As they watched, Johnny Sharp collected his breakfast plate and took it to a table, where he sat alone. Clint could see Tina watching him from her table, and Carlos watching Tina. He definitely knew of his young wife's interest in the marksman.

"Do you want to go over and meet him now?" Emmy asked.

"Let him eat his breakfast," Clint said. "Besides, I'm sure he knows I'm sitting over here. Maybe he'll make the move to meet *me*."

"There's one thing you got to remember about Johnny," Bizzy said. "He's young, and he's cocky."

"Is he a friend of yours?" Clint asked.

"No," Bizzy said. "I don't like cocky youngsters. I'd like to see you take him down a peg."

"I'm not looking to do that, or to take his spot as headliner," Clint said.

"Did the Count already offer it to you?" Bizzy asked.

"He mentioned it."

"And you didn't say yes?"

"I didn't," Clint said. "I told him I'd think about it."

"But you're gonna meet Johnny before you decide, right?" Emmy asked.

"Just between you and me," he said to Emmy, "I'm not interested in being a performer."

"Then whatta you doin' here?" Bizzy asked. "After you helped us with the wagon you coulda went on your way."

"And miss out on seeing a place called Freakville?" Clint asked. "My curiosity got the better of me, and it still is."

"What do you think so far?" Emmy asked.

"All the folks I've met are . . . interesting," Clint said.

"There's a lot of talent, here," Emmy said.

"What about Electro, over there?" Clint asked. "Is he really electrically charged?"

"He's been hit by lightning three times," Bizzy said, "and he's still alive. Whatta you think?"

Clint continued to watch Emmy and Bizzy eat, while casting an eye over at Johnny every so often.

"Looks like he's almost done," Bizzy said. "Think he's gonna come over here?"

"If he's as cocky as you say—"

"Cocky, but also arrogant," Bizzy said. "My guess is he'll wait for you."

"I think so, too," Emmy said.

"Then maybe you'll walk over there with me and introduce us," he said to Emmy.

"That's what I've been waitin' to do," she said. "Now?"

"Now's as good a time as any," Clint said, and they both stood up.

***

Johnny Sharp ate his food at a slow, steady pace and tried not to seem as if he was looking over at Clint Adams. The man was a legend, and it would be easy to allow him to intimidate a younger man, but Johnny was determined to avoid that. He knew how good he was with a gun. He had never missed anything he shot at, whether it was a bullseye or a two-bit piece.

He had spotted Clint Adams as soon as he entered but controlled himself. Rather than walk right over and challenge him, he decided to let the Gunsmith come to him.

And here he came.

Chapter Sixteen

Emmy and Clint reached Johnny Sharp's table. The young man continued to eat.

"Johnny," Emmy said, "this Clint Adams. Clint, meet Johnny Sharp."

Johnny finished cutting a piece of steak, stuck it in his mouth, and then looked up at Clint and Emmy.

"Thanks for the introduction, Emmy," he said. "Siddown, Adams."

"Mister Adams," Clint said.

"What?"

"A young man like you should show the proper respect for his elders," Clint said. "Call me Mister Adams."

Sharp sat back in his chair and stared up at Clint for a few moments.

"Why don't you have a seat, Mister Adams."

"Thanks," Clint said, "I believe I will."

He sat across from the young man, still holding his coffee cup in his left hand.

"Don't let me interrupt your breakfast."

"I won't," Sharp said, "and I won't let you interrupt my life, either."

"I don't plan to."

"I'm the headliner, here," Sharp said, "no matter what anybody's told you."

"That's what I heard."

"Then why are you still here?"

"This is a very interesting place," Clint said. "And I understand you shoot pretty good."

"I shoot perfectly."

"I'd like to see that."

Sharp put down his knife and fork and stared at Clint.

"You wanna shoot against me?"

"I didn't say that," Clint replied. "I want to see you shoot. I'm always interested in people who know how to use a gun."

"Oh, I know how."

"How did you learn?"

"I picked up a gun when I was fifteen," Sharp said. "The first time I fired it, I hit what I was aiming at."

"Ah, a natural, huh?"

"I guess so," Sharp said. "Over the last ten years I just got better and better."

"And then the Count saw you shoot," Clint said.

"Yes."

"Well, I'd like to see you shoot."

"I think the Count wants us to shoot against each other," Sharp said.

"Let's leave him out of it, for now," Clint suggested. "I'm telling you I don't want your job. I'd just like to see you shoot."

"I made myself a shooting gallery just outside of town. Nothing fancy, just some bottles and cans, and a bullseye. We can go there." Sharp started to stand.

"Easy," Clint said. "Finish your breakfast first, and then we'll go."

While the young man ate, Clint thought he wasn't seeing the arrogance he had been told about. The young man just seemed to want to show him what he had, now that Clint had assured him he didn't want his job.

***

Clint followed Johnny Sharp out of town to his makeshift shooting gallery. There were shards of shattered glass and mangled cans scattered around the base of a wooden fence, and a bullseye with many holes in the center.

"I'll set up some cans and bottles," Sharp said.

He ran to the fence, found some bottles that hadn't been broken yet, and some fairly solid cans and then set them on top of the fence.

He ran back to join Clint and said, "I usually shoot from about a hundred feet."

"Go ahead," Clint said.

The boy set his feet, dropped his hands to his side, then drew and fired six times. Three bottles shattered, and three cans jumped. He turned to Clint for approval.

"Not bad," Clint said. "Can you do a hundred yards?"

Sharp looked behind him, then said, "Sure."

He set up some cans and bottles again, then they walked back until Clint figured they were a hundred yards off.

"Any time you're ready," he said.

Johnny Sharp set himself again, then drew and fired six times, hitting a target all six times.

"Can you hit a moving target?"

"Sure," Sharp said again.

Clint walked to the fence, looked around, found a couple of whiskey bottles, and grabbed a few cans, then returned to where Sharp was standing.

"I'll toss these into the air, you hit them before they hit the ground."

"No problem."

Clint waited for the young man to reload, then tossed each bottle and can into the air, quickly, one after the other. Sharp drew and fired, shattering both bottles and puncturing both cans.

"That's good. Let's try something else."

Clint picked up one of the cans while Sharp reloaded.

"Let's see how many times you can hit this can before it touches the ground."

"Right."

Clint tossed the can up. Sharp drew and fired six times, each bullet struck the can, keeping it in the air. The only reason it fell to earth was because Sharp was out of bullets.

"That's damn good shooting," Clint admitted.

"Thanks, Mister Adams," Sharp said.

"Just call me Clint, kid."

Chapter Seventeen

"Let's try something smaller," Clint suggested.

"Like what?"

Clint took a two-bit piece from his pocket.

"Can you hit this if I toss it in the air?"

Sharp hesitated, then said, "Yeah, I can."

Clint noticed that Sharp carried a double-action 1877 Colt Peacemaker, the same kind Doc Holliday carried. Clint's was an older model, formerly a single-action which he converted into double-action even before Colt instituted the feature.

"I'm going to toss it into the air," Clint said. "See if you can hit it."

"Right."

Clint tossed the coin up. It flipped over and over, catching the sunlight, and as it reached its zenith Johnny Sharp fired. The coin fell to the ground. Clint trotted over and picked it up, looked at it, then held it up.

"Dead center!" he called out. He walked back to where Sharp was standing. "Not bad, kid."

"Not bad?" Sharp repeated. "Can you do it?"

"You're doing the shooting today, kid, not me."

"Come on," Sharp said, grabbing the punctured coin from Clint's hand. "Show me what you got."

Without hesitating, Sharp tossed the coin in the air, sure he was catching the Gunsmith flatfooted.

Clint drew quickly and fired once. The coin came down and Sharp ran over to pick it up and inspect it.

"Ha!" he yelled. "You missed."

He ran back to Clint and held the coin up.

"There's only my hole."

"Look again," Clint said, reloading.

"Whataya mean?"

"I mean look real closely at that coin."

Sharp held the coin up and squinted at it. He saw the hole his bullet had made, but then he saw what Clint was talking about.

"There's a nick—" He stopped and looked at Clint. "Your bullet went through the hole I made?"

Clint didn't say anything.

"Come on," Sharp said, "show me somethin' else."

"Okay," Clint relented. He took a deck of cards from his pocket—a used deck he played solitaire with to kill time—fanned through it and removed all the sixes. Then he put the rest back in his pocket.

He walked to the fence, wedged the four cards into the top, and walked back. Then he turned, drew and fired six times, quickly.

"Take a look," he said.

Sharp ran to the fence, grabbed a card and came back while Clint was reloading. He held up the six of spades, only all six of the spades on the card had been punctured.

"Okay," Clint said, "now you do the six of hearts."

Sharp assumed his stance, squinted, then drew and fired, not quite as quickly as Clint had.

Clint went to the fence, grabbed the six of hearts and carried it back. He held it up so Sharp could see it. There were six holes where the hearts used to be.

"You gonna say that's 'not bad?' " the kid asked. "I did what you did."

"Yeah, you did," Clint said, "but you could've done it faster."

"Okay," Sharp said, holstering his gun, "this time we'll shoot together. You take clubs, I'll take diamonds."

"You got it," Clint agreed.

They stood side-by-side, giving each other plenty of room to draw.

"Say when," Sharp said.

"On three," Clint said. "one . . . two . . . three."

They both drew and fired six times. Anyone listening would swear there were only six shots fired, not twelve. They were that close together.

Sharp ran to the fence to claim both cards and carry them back. He held them both up. The clubs and diamonds were all gone.

"You got anythin' else?" Johnny Sharp asked.

"One more thing," Clint said.

Sharp pocketed the cards and said, "What?"

Clint reached into his pocket and took out two Lucifer matchsticks.

"I'm going to put two of these on that fence. We each have to light one with a single shot."

"You done this before?" Sharp asked, surprised

"A time or two," Clint said. "You've got to have good eyesight, perfect accuracy. My friend Bill Hickok used to do this, before his eyesight started to fail."

"Okay," Sharp said, "I guess if it was good enough for Wild Bill Hickok it's good enough for me."

Clint walked to the fence, jammed the matches into the top, about five feet apart, then walked back.

"It doesn't matter who fires first," Clint said. "You just have to light the match. Got it?"

"I got it."

"Whenever you're ready."

Clint was letting the kid call the play, so Sharp got to draw first. After they had each fired, they both walked to the fence.

Clint's match head had been lit. Sharp's match had been chopped off, half of it still stuck in the fence.

"I hit it!" Sharp said.

"But you didn't light it."

Sharp looked on the ground frantically, finally came up with the other half of his match. The head was still intact.

"But I hit it," he pointed out, again. "That's good shootin'."

"It is," Clint said, "but the object was to light the match, not just hit it. But don't worry, kid, you're good."

Clint reloaded, holstered his gun and walked away.

Chapter Eighteen

It had been an interesting afternoon.

He hadn't meant to show the kid up, he'd just intended to watch him shoot. But Sharp had pretty much challenged him. Walking off after the match shot was his way of making a statement. He didn't know how Johnny Sharp was going to react to their afternoon shoot-out, but that would just be one more interesting thing about his visit to Freakville.

The mess tent seemed to be the gathering place in town, since there were no restaurants or saloons, so Clint returned there. With fifty or sixty people in Freakville, there wasn't seating enough for everyone, so it seemed the populace ate in shifts. There was a whole new group, waiting in line or sitting and eating when he arrived.

Clint got himself yet another cup of coffee—he really could have used a beer—and looked around. He saw a man seated at a table, eating. He not only had a knife and fork, but there were two swords on the table.

"Excuse me," Clint said to a normal looking worker, "what's he do with those swords?"

The man looked to where Clint was pointing, and said, "Oh, that's Lance. He's a sword swallower."

"Swallower?"

"Yep," the man said, "he swallows 'em. I dunno how he does it, but he does."

"I'd like to see that."

"Just ask 'im," the man said "He'll do it for ya. But you gotta see Flamo."

"Who's Flamo?"

"He ain't in here, right now," the man said, "but he eats fire."

"Thanks," Clint said. The man nodded and left the tent.

There were obviously a lot more interesting people for him to meet.

***

Johnny Sharp banged on the door of the Count's house. It was finally answered by Belle. She was wearing a lavender robe with fur trim, knotted at her trim waist, but Sharp didn't seem to notice.

"Johnny!" she said. "What are you doing here?"

"Belle," he said, "I gotta see the Count."

"He's eating breakfast."

"This late?" It was almost noon.

"We were, uh, kind of busy, this morning," Belle said.

"Ask 'im if he'll see me," Sharp said, "please?"

She relented with a sigh.

"Come on in."

She closed the door and led him to the dining room, where the Count was sitting at the head of a long table. He was wearing a red robe and a satisfied smile.

"Johnny!" he greeted. "Come join me. Belle, pour Johnny some coffee."

Johnny sat heavily and ignored the cup of coffee Belle set in front of him.

"What's wrong?" the Count asked. "You look like somebody killed your cat."

"I—I went shootin' with Clint Adams."

The Count's good mood vanished.

"Why did you do that?"

"We met in the mess tent, and he said he wanted to see me shoot."

"Where'd you go?"

"Outside of town, where I usually practice."

"And nobody saw you?"

"No," Sharp said, "no one."

"That's good," the Count said. "Now, tell me everything that happened."

***

Clint carried his coffee over to Lance's table.

"Hi," he said, "I'm Clint Adams."

"I know," Lance said. "The Gunsmith. I'm Lancelot. Everybody calls me Lance. Join me?"

"Thanks."

Lance was an extremely handsome man in his thirties. He appeared to be a perfect match for Belle.

But Clint had sat down for another reason. He looked at the swords.

"I'm told you swallow those."

"That's right."

"Isn't that . . . difficult?" Clint asked. "And dangerous?"

"Not if you know what you're doing," Lance said. He poked at his plate with his fork. "Sometimes it's easier to swallow a sword than this steak."

"Mine was very good this morning."

"This one is well done," Lance said. "Takes a lot of chewing."

Clint looked at the two swords, one straight and the other curved.

"I've never seen one like that," he said, pointing.

"Ah," Lance said, "that's a scimitar." He touched the jewel encrusted handle. "It's my favorite."

"I'd love to see what you do," Clint said.

"I've got to finish this steak," Lance said, "but I'll be rehearsing in a couple of hours in the big tent. Meet me there and you can watch."

"Thanks," Clint said. "I'll do that."

Lance picked up his utensils and attacked his well-done steak.

Chapter Nineteen

"A match?" the Count said.

Sharp nodded.

"And he lit it?" Belle said.

"Hey," Sharp said, "I hit it."

"But the object was to light it," the Count pointed out. "So he outshot you."

"This time," Sharp said. "It won't happen again. I hit all the other targets he hit." He didn't mention the two-bit piece.

"I told you not to shoot with him until you heard from me," the Count said.

"Hey," Sharp said, "he came over to me, said he wanted to see me shoot."

"Fine," the Count said, "you should've shown him a couple of things and let it go at that. You didn't have to shoot it out with him."

"What do we do now?"

"I have to assess the damage you've done," the Count said. "Just stay away from him until you hear from me."

"Yeah, okay."

"Show him out, Belle."

Belle obeyed, leading Sharp to the front door, where he turned to her and lowered his voice.

"When can I see you?"

"I'll let you know," she said. "Right now, he needs me."

"To go after Adams?"

"Don't you worry about it," she said, touching his cheek. "We'll be together soon."

"If you pick Adams over me . . ." Sharp said, his tone threatening.

"My dear boy," she said, "I'm only going to do what the Count asks me to."

She ushered him out the door before he could say something stupid.

As she reentered the dining room the Count asked, "Do you have control of him?"

"Of course."

"Then he'll stay away from Adams from now on?"

"Don't worry, darling," Belle said, "just leave Johnny and Adams to me."

The Count put some butter on a piece of bread and said, "You know I'm close. All we need is the Gunsmith to put us over the top."

She walked around behind him and put her hands on his shoulders.

"How many men have you known to resist me?" she asked.

"None," he said, "and that includes me."

Abruptly, he turned his chair sideways so she could go on her knees in front of him. She undid his trousers, and a raging cock sprang forward. She caressed it with her hands, cooed to it, rubbed it against her cheek, and finally engulfed it in her hot mouth. The Count sighed and let his head drop back as she sucked him . . .

***

Johnny Sharp stopped outside the house, and rather than walk away, thought about peering in a window. Nobody in Freakville knew exactly what the relationship was between the Count and Belle. He didn't like the thought of the Count taking Belle into his bed. He knew all of the men in town were in love with Belle, but she said she was in love with him. Of course, she could have been lying, but he didn't like that thought, either.

In the end, he decided to walk away and not take a look. If he didn't like what he saw, it could cause a problem between him and the Count. And there was already a potential problem—Clint Adams—so why add to it?

***

After she finished the Count off, he returned to his breakfast, Belle went to clean up and get dressed. She didn't believe Johnny Sharp was going to be a problem, but Clint Adams was another matter. In the short time she had spent with him, she found him to be different from any other man she had known. For one thing, he did not instantly fall in love with her. That was unusual. So now she was going to have to bring all of her powers to bear on him. It would be a challenge, one she had never had to deal with before.

***

The Count was concerned.

Belle's ministrations had relaxed his body but done nothing to calm the turmoil in his mind. He needed to concentrate on convincing Clint Adams to join the show, or there might not even be a show. All of the freaks in Freakville had confidence in him, but lately, his own confidence had been waning somewhat. The arrival of the Gunsmith appeared to be a Godsend, but it remained to be seen if he was going to be able to take advantage of it.

He buttered another piece of bread.

Chapter Twenty

When Clint entered the big top tent where he had played poker with Smilin' Jack and the others, he found there were more performers rehearsing than just the sword swallower, Lance.

Off to one side he saw a man holding several torches and assumed this was the fire-eater he'd been told about. In another area the six-fingered juggler, Lefty, was tossing things into the air. But Clint's interest was still in the sword swallower, so he walked over to Lance.

"Came to watch, huh?" Lance asked.

"I've got to," Clint said. "I can't imagine how you do this."

"I can't tell you how," Lance said. "I can just show you."

"I'll just be quiet and watch."

First Lance took the longer sword, which to Clint looked like what officers in the Civil War had carried, a saber. Lance took the sword, held it over his head, tilted his head up and opened his mouth. Clint flinched as the man stuck the tip of the sword into his mouth and then just kept going. He only stopped when he got to the hilt.

The entire blade was now engulfed. After a few moments, he grasped the hilt and slid the blade out.

He set the sabre aside and picked up the curved scimitar.

"Have you ever read Arabian Nights?" he asked Clint.

"As a matter of fact, I have," Clint said. "But I've never seen a scimitar before. Doesn't the curve make that, uh, trickier?"

"You'd think so, wouldn't you?" Lance asked.

He did the same thing with this blade, raised it, tilted his head and slid the blade in. Clint couldn't help but flinch again as the blade disappeared. After a few moments, Lance slid the blade back out.

"What happens if you catch cold," he asked, "and get a sore throat."

"Believe it or not," Lance said, "the swords help."

"That's just amazing," Clint said.

"How'd you like to see the fire-eater? Flamo?"

"I would."

"Come on."

Lance led the way across the tent to where the flame-eater was rehearsing. As they watched, the man held a torch to his mouth, seemed to swallow the flame and then spit it back out. He did the same with the second torch, then looked at Clint and Lance. He appeared to be in his fifties and wore a turban on his head with a blue jewel in it. This was the man Clint would have thought would be swallowing scimitars.

But no, his desert of preference was fire.

"How does he do that without burning his mouth?" Clint wondered.

"He can't tell you that any more than I can tell you how I swallow swords," Lance said.

"You're both unbelievable," Clint said.

"Would you like to see Gordo rehearse?" Lance asked. "He lefts heavy weights, bends iron bars."

"No, that's okay," Clint said. "I think I've seen enough for one day."

"Then I'll go back to rehearsing, if you don't mind," Lance said.

"Sure," Clint said, "thanks for taking the time to show me around."

Clint was heading for the tent entrance when Belle appeared. She was dressed in a peach-colored dress that showed off her smooth shoulders, and the upper slope of her full breasts. All of the men rehearsing in the tent stopped to look at her.

"There you are," she said. "I've been looking for you."

"You found me," Clint said. "What's on your mind?"

"Take a walk with me?"

"Always," he said.

They left the tent together.

"Where are we going?" Clint asked, as they continued on.

"Somewhere we can talk," she said, "privately."

"Your house?"

She smiled.

"I think you know by now that wasn't my house," she said. "People talk."

"Yes, they do."

"I know these freaks talk about me and the Count," she said. "And he knows it."

"Do either of you care?"

"Not really," she said. "Our relationship is our business."

"You mean his business, don't you?" Clint asked. "Tell me, what shows has he had before? And just what is he the Count of?"

She laughed.

"Probably nothing," she said. "It's a title, really. And one that he gave himself. Then again, he could have dubbed himself king."

"And would that make you his queen?"

"I'm neither queen nor countess," she said. "I'm just . . . Belle."

"The witch."

"One of two witches," she said. "I'm sure you've heard about Kyra."

"Just her name, nothing more," Clint said. "Oh, and that she's neither black nor white."

"Kyra is an entity all her own," Belle said. "But she's not what I wanted to talk about."

"What then?" he asked.

"Not here," she said, looking around them. "Too many ears." She linked her arm into his left. "Come this way."

Chapter Twenty-One

Belle walked Clint to a deserted part of town. He had to wonder if she was leading him into some kind of trap. But so far, no one in Freakville displayed any animosity toward him. So he assumed she had something she wanted to discuss in complete confidence.

"There's nobody in this part of town," she said. "That's why I like it here. This building used to be a saloon."

She took him to the entrance, where the batwing doors were hanging by a single hinge each. Inside were some tables and chairs that were mostly in pieces, but one table and two chairs had been set up in the center of the room.

"Let's sit," she said.

When he was seated across from her she said, "I usually come here alone, to think. Today I brought you here so I can warn you."

"Warn me about what?"

"The Count," she said. "He wants to use you."

"I know that, Belle," he said. "He sent you to convince me."

"Johnny came and told us you outshot him."

"Not by much," Clint said. "He's got some talent with a gun."

"You should also know," she said, "that there's another show being put together in Flagstaff by someone the Count considers an enemy."

"Who's that?"

"His name is Angus McDougal. He calls himself The Irishman. Both he and the Count intend to travel the West with their show, the way Buffalo Bill Cody does. But he's in Europe now, so both the Count and the Irishman want to fill his boots. They'll do whatever they can to beat each other. As soon as you came to town, the Count figured he had the edge."

"This is all very interesting," Clint said. "But it doesn't change anything. I don't have any desire to be part of a traveling circus, or Wild West Show, or whatever the Count is going to call it. Cody's a friend of mine, and I wouldn't do it for him."

"So if the Irishman came to you, you'd say no?"

"Definitely."

"I can tell the Count that?"

"Sure, go ahead," Clint said.

"Well," she said, "there's something else we should get out of the way while we're here."

"What's that?"

She stood up, reached behind her and undid the peach-colored dress she was wearing. It slid off her very easily and fell to the floor. Obviously, she had planned this, for she was completely naked underneath.

"Belle," Clint said, "I have to warn you, I'm not going to fall in love with you like all the other men here. No matter how you try to bewitch me."

"Oh, I know that," she said. "I knew it as soon as we met. But I'm not trying to make you fall in love with me. I just want you to make love to me."

"Here?" he asked. "It's kind of dusty, and anybody could come along."

"Right here on this table will do fine," she said, "and nobody ever comes here."

Her breasts were large, pear-shaped, with large, dark nipples. She was a full-bodied woman with lovely smooth skin and opulent curves. He wasn't going to fall in love with her, but damn it, he wanted her. How could he not?

"Whatever you say, Belle."

He came around the table, took her into his arms and kissed her. She pressed her hot body tightly against him. He ran his hands over that smooth as silk skin.

"Right here," she said, backing away until she butted up against the table. "But you have too many clothes on."

He unstrapped his gun and set it nearby, on a chair, then started taking off the rest of his clothes. He hopped around on one foot, then the other to get his boots off, then removed his trousers. When he was naked, she fell to her knees in front of him, took his hard, jutting cock into her hands. She stroked it for a short while before taking it into her mouth. She was very talented, using her hands, tongue and lips to bring him to the brink before releasing him.

She stood up and rested her butt on the table. He went to her, took her in his arms and kissed her again, then laid her down on the table. He didn't know if the table would hold their weight, so he simply leaned over her and began to explore her body with his hands and mouth. Pendulous when she was standing, her large breasts fell to either side a bit when she was lying on her back. But they were firm in his hands and mouth, and her nipples were distended. She gasped as he worked his way down until he was crouched in front of the table with his face in her crotch. Her legs were dangling over the edge, but he took them and lifted them onto his shoulders. Then he began to devour her . . .

Chapter Twenty-Two

After Belle left his house, the Count finished his breakfast and left the table for her to clean when she came back. Belle was not only the white witch in his show, she was his housekeeper, his whore, his property. The hold he had on her enabled him to use her any way he saw fit.

He poured himself an after-breakfast glass of brandy, drank it standing up. Johnny Sharp had annoyed him. The arrogant youngster might have ruined things with the Gunsmith. The Count just hoped Belle would be able to work her magic on Clint Adams. So far, the only man the Count had ever seen resist Belle's charms was himself. He wasn't in love with her, he just owned her.

He stopped thinking about Belle, and Adams, and Johnny Sharp, and started thinking about the Irishman. He had gotten word from a contact in Flagstaff that McDougal was close to launching his show. If the Irishman did, indeed, get his show off the ground first, then the Count was truly going to need the Gunsmith. He wouldn't be able to fight the Irishman any other way.

Unless, of course, something happened to him. After all, no Irishman, no show.

The Count poured a second brandy and considered that option.

***

When Clint was ready to enter Belle, they tested the strength of the table. Rather than crawl atop her, he pulled her to the edge of the table so he could drive himself into her while standing. Still, as he pounded away at her, fucking her for all he was worth, that table creaked and moved beneath them.

She gasped and cried out, reaching for him, but couldn't get her hands on him, so she gripped the table on either side of her and when he exploded into her, she screamed . . .

Moments later, still lying naked on the tabletop, she said, "You have a bit of magic of your own, don't you?"

"Well," he said, pulling up his trousers, "it's never been called that before, but I'll take it."

Slowly she rolled on to her side and slid off the table. As he finished dressing and strapped on his gunbelt, she pulled her dress back on, straightened it out, then patted herself.

"So tell me," she said, "are you in love with me?"

"I'm afraid not, Belle," he said. "What we just did was pure lust."

She laughed.

"I was just checking," she said. "Oh, another warning."

"Yes?"

"You can't let anyone find out what we just did," she said. "We don't want it to get back to the Count."

"Isn't this what he sent you after me to do?" he asked.

"Not quite," she said. "Make you fall in love with me, yes. Fuck me, no."

"So you're playing with fire?" Clint asked. "What if he finds out?"

"I could probably handle him," she said.

Clint studied Belle, wondering who had the upper hand in their relationship, her or the Count. After all, he was apparently the man in charge.

"We better head back to the populated part of town," Belle said. We don't want folks wondering where we got off to and what we're doing."

"You don't think they know?"

"They might think they know," she said. "But there's no point in confirming their suspicions."

They left the saloon and started walking toward the center of town.

"Let's part ways here," she said, before they reached a populated street. "I'll head back to the Count's house. He's going to want me to clean up after his breakfast."

"Are you his cook and housekeeper, too?" Clint asked.

"I'm a lot of things, Clint," she said. "I'll see you later."

He watched her walk away. He knew he wasn't in love with her, but it sounded like she was almost a slave to the Count. He would have liked to help her.

He turned and headed back toward the mess tent. His time with Belle had made him hungry.

***

As usual, the mess tent was about half-full with people dining or waiting in line for their food. One of the people who always seemed to be eating was Emmy and, as usual, at a table by herself.

Clint got himself some coffee and went to her table.

"Do you mind?" he asked.

"Why would I mind?" she asked. "You're the only person who ever wants to sit with me."

"I'm always happy to sit with you, Emmy," he said, smiling and sitting across from her. "You're the nicest person I've met here."

"That's a sweet thing to say," she said, "but you still haven't met everyone. In fact, I was going to look for you today." She glanced around, then leaned in to whisper. "There's somebody who wants to meet you."

"Oh? Who's that?"

"You finish your coffee," she said, "I'll finish my snack, and then I'll take you."

From the amount of food in front of her, her snack would take a while to finish.

Chapter Twenty-Three

"Somebody actually lives here?" Clint asked, when they stopped in front of a small house.

"Yes," Emmy said. "Why?"

"Oh, it's just the last time somebody told me they lived in a house here in town, it turned out to be empty."

"That'd be Belle," Emmy said, wryly. "She thinks people believe her."

"So who lives here?"

"You'll find out," she said. "Just go to the door and knock."

"If I didn't trust you, Emmy," he said, "I'd think you were sending me into some kind of trap."

"You trust me?" she asked.

"I do," he said. "I told you, you're the nicest person I've met here. I'll believe anything you tell me."

Tears formed in her eyes.

"Nobody's been so kind to me in . . . well, ever!" she said. She leaned over, because if she tried to get close to him, she'd bump him with her big body. Instead, she simply kissed him on the cheek.

"It's no trap," she told him.

"Okay, then."

He walked to the front door and knocked. The woman who answered was long and lean, with long blonde hair and an angular, yet beautiful face. The black dress she wore clung to her, showing off her very slim waist and small, peach-sized breasts. Her skin was pale and smooth, and her eyes were a beguiling grey.

"Mr. Adams?" she asked.

"That's right."

"Thank you for coming," she said. "I'm Kyra."

Ah, he thought, the other witch in town.

"I know what you're thinking," she said. "Yes, I am the other witch in town. Please come in."

He wasn't impressed. She could've guessed what was going through his mind.

"Thank you."

He entered the small house, found it well furnished with a sofa, armchairs, a table and chairs—in fact, the house was cramped with furnishings.

"Yes, the house was like this when I found it and decided to move in," she said. "May I offer you some tea? It's my own blend. It not only tastes good, but it's good for the body and the soul. I'm sure one of yours must need some help. Body or soul?"

"I don't know about that," he said, "but yes, I'll have some tea."

"Good," she said. "Please sit. I'll only be a minute or two."

She left the room, presumably to go into the kitchen. When she returned, she was carrying a silver tray with a pot and two cups.

Clint had taken a seat on the sofa, and she sat next to him, setting the tray down on the table in front of them.

"Sugar? Cream?"

"I'll just take it black, thanks."

"Very good," she said. "That's how it should be consumed."

She poured the dark looking tea into a cup and handed it to him. For a moment he stared into it, wondering what effect it might have on him.

"Don't worry," she said, "it really is just tea. It won't put a spell on you."

He sipped it, found it aromatic and flavorful.

"Is it all right?" she asked.

"It's very good," he said. "Thank you."

She smiled, poured a cup for herself. In profile her nose came to a slight point, as did her chin. She was not classically beautiful, but lovely just the same. Her blonde hair was parted in the center, fell straight down past her shoulders.

"I'm sure you're wondering why I asked Emmy to bring you here?" she said.

"The thought had crossed my mind."

"Well, you've already met many of the freaks in town," she said. "I thought it was time we met. I'm sure you've heard the talk."

"The talk?"

"About me," she said. "My witchcraft, as opposed to Belle's."

"Well," he said, "I have been told that Belle is the white witch in town, but I'm sure that doesn't make you, uh—"

"I don't believe in those labels," she said. "I believe Belle and I are witches, plain and simple, but from different covens."

"Covens?"

"A coven is a group of witches who form—well, we can call it, a family. It's not a widely used word."

"So there are others like the two of you?"

"Oh yes," she said, "just not here. But all over the country and, of course, across Europe."

"I see."

"Belle and I were born in this country," she said, "but that is all we have in common."

"Well, not all."

"How so?"

"You both want to be in the Count's show."

"Yes, the Count," she said. "I'm afraid you must be made aware of just who and what the Count is."

"And you're going to tell me?"

"Oh, yes, indeed," she said. "I am."

Chapter Twenty-Four

"What do you mean, who and what he is?" Clint asked. "I thought he was, like, the ringmaster, or something."

"That's what he wants to be," Kyra said.

Clint noticed a heady scent about Kyra but fought to keep his own head clear. Her beauty may not have been as blatantly intoxicating as Belle's, but her presence was.

He put his teacup down on the table and turned to look into her eyes.

"So," he said, "tell me. Just who is the Count?"

"He's the Devil."

"The Devil," Clint said. "You mean like, Satan? From the Catholic church?"

"It's not only Catholics who believe in the Devil," she told him. "In fact, he doesn't only exist in religion."

"So you're telling me Satan is real," Clint said, "and he's the Count."

She warmed to her subject.

"I'm not talking about the red man with the horns," she said. "That's just something that was made up to scare children."

"Uh-huh."

"No," she said, "I'm talking about evil, pure evil."

"And that's the Count?" Clint said. "What evil is he trying to perform by putting together a traveling circus?"

She moved even closer to Clint, so that their hips were almost touching.

"Who goes to the circus, Mr. Adams?"

"Families," he said.

"That's right," she said. "Children. He will have access to hundreds, maybe thousands of children."

"Then why are you here in Freakville, Kyra?" Clint asked. "Why do you want to be part of his show?"

"To stop him," she said. "To prevent him from spreading his evil."

"And why are you telling me this?"

"Because he's trying to recruit you," she said. "I'm, warning you. You don't want to be part of his show."

"No, I don't," Clint said. "I know that."

"Then why are you still here?" she asked. "Is it Belle? Has she already spread her legs for you?"

He wondered if she could see the answer on his face.

"That's not it, at all," he said. "I just find this place interesting. All of it. "Lance, Flamo, Emmy, Bizzy, Belle, and even you. It's all interesting."

She sat back and regarded him silently for a moment, then picked up her own tea and sipped it.

"So how long do you intend to stay?"

"I don't know," he said. "I've already been here longer than I thought I would be."

"Because of Belle?"

"No."

"You're not in love with her?"

"No."

"But have you been with her?"

"No!" he lied.

"You have to be careful of the Count," she said. "He owns Belle."

"But not you?" he asked.

"No," she said, "not me." She put her teacup down. "Thank you for coming to see me, Mr. Adams."

"I did it because Emmy asked me to," he said, as they walked to the door.

"Emmy is sweet," she said, "but be careful you don't fall into bed with her. Her husband is very jealous."

"I know that," Clint said. "They were the first people I met from here."

As they got to the door he turned and asked, "Tell me, is there anyone else in this town who believes that the Count is the Devil?"

"You want to confirm what I've told you?"

"I'm just checking," he said.

"Talk to Bizzy," Kyra said. "He knows everyone."

She closed the door before he could ask anything else.

***

Clint headed back to the more populated area of Freakville, thinking about the witch, Kyra, and everything she had told him. He was pleased she hadn't tried to convince him that the Count actually was Satan, but simply meant that the man was evil. Clint had no personal opinion on whether or not this was true. He hadn't spent enough time with the man to form an opinion. But he was thinking he probably should do what Kyra suggested and talk to Bizzy.

The little man seemed to have a mind of his own and would probably speak the truth. Of course, he might have to use Emmy to get her husband to actually talk with him. It was very clear that Bizzy didn't like him.

So far, the feeling was mutual.

Chapter Twenty-Five

For a change Emmy wasn't in the mess tent, so Clint walked over to the rehearsal big top. He didn't know what kind of rehearsing she needed to do to be the fat lady, but sure enough, she was there.

She was sitting off to one side watching some of the rehearsals. Clint walked over, grabbed a chair and sat down next to her.

"Did Kyra put a spell on you?" she asked.

"No," he said, "she just wanted to warn me."

"About what?"

"The Count."

Emmy looked at him.

"About what?"

"She says he's evil," Clint said, "he's the Devil."

"My God."

"She also told me there's somebody else in town who feels the same way."

"Who?"

"Bizzy."

"What?"

"Do you think you can get him to talk to me?"

"I've never heard Bizzy say that about the Count," she said, "but I can get him to talk to you."

"Are you sure?" Clint asked. "He doesn't like me."

Emmy laughed.

"Bizzy doesn't like anybody," she said. "Just let me talk to him. I'll let you know tonight."

"Okay," he said. "Thanks."

"What did you think of Kyra?" Emmy asked.

"She's . . . different."

"She's beautiful, don't you think?" Emmy asked.

"Belle's beautiful," Clint said. "Kyra is . . . I don't know, special."

"So she did put a spell on you."

"If you're asking if I'm in love with her after one meeting, the answer is no."

"I like Kyra," Emmy said.

"And Belle?"

She made a face.

"I hate Belle."

"That's too bad."

"Naw," Emmy said, "she doesn't care."

"Where should I meet you later?" he asked, standing.

She smiled.

"Where do you think?"

"Mess tent it is," he said, and left the big top.

***

Clint went back to his room, sat on the bed and wondered why he didn't just leave town? He'd met a lot of interesting people, but now he was getting into something that really wasn't his business. Yet he still felt a need to at least talk to Bizzy and see what the little man had to say.

For want of something better to do, he sat back on the bed, his back to the wall, and closed his eyes, still wearing his gun, and dozed off . . .

He woke with a start, from a dream about a devil chasing him with a pitchfork. A check of the time told him he had been asleep for fifteen minutes. He took the dream as a sign that he should pursue what Kyra told him. The first step would be to talk with Bizzy.

He stood up, washed his face in the basin, and left the room.

***

He considered talking to the other oddities he had met—Jack, Lance, Flamo, even Gordo—about what Kyra had told him, but put that aside until he could meet with Bizzy.

As he entered the mess tent, he not only saw Emmy seated at a table, eating, but Bizzy, as well. The little man had a sour look on his face as he ate.

Clint approached the table where Emmy and her husband were seated.

"There you are," Emmy said. "I'm going to take my plate to another table so you two can talk."

As she walked away Bizzy said, "You ever see anybody eat as much as she does?"

"Never," Clint said. "It's . . . impressive."

"They're makin' steaks today," Bizzy said. "Go and get yourself one. We don't want people wonderin' why we're sittin' together if you're not eatin'."

"I get it," Clint said. He went and got in line, returned with a full steak dinner on his plate.

"Cooked to perfection, ain't it?" Bizzy asked. "Nice and bloody."

"Yes," Clint said, "it's perfect."

"Okay," Bizzy said, "Emmy said you wanted to talk to me. About what?"

"About something Kyra told me earlier today," Clint said.

"Kyra, that witch!" Bizzy said. "What'd she tell you?"

"Something she said you would confirm," Clint answered. "That the Count is the Devil."

Bizzy frowned.

"That big mouth bitch."

Chapter Twenty-Six

"What did Kyra tell ya?" Bizzy asked.

"That the Count is evil," Clint answered. "Well, what she said was that he's the Devil. That he wants to spread his evil by using his traveling show."

"Why does it matter what he wants to do?" Bizzy asked. "He's gonna give a lot of people jobs."

"Kyra told me you're the only other person who knows about him," Clint said. "How do you know him so well?"

"We worked together before," Bizzy said.

"When?"

"Oh, years ago," Bizzy said.

"Where?"

"That doesn't matter."

"So then Kyra's right," Clint said. "You know the man."

Bizzy nodded.

"And how many of these others did you know before getting here?"

"He contacted all of these people and got them to come here with the promise of puttin' them in a big show. The only ones I knew before they came here were Emmy and Kyra."

"So you can back her story, then," Clint said.

"I probably could," Bizzy said, "but why should I?"

"To keep him from spreading his evil."

"What's it matter if he spreads it?" Bizzy asked. "Look at all the people he's puttin' to work. Where else do you think they could get jobs?"

"Yeah, but if she's right—"

"What's your interest, anyway?" Bizzy asked, cutting him off. "Why do you care?"

Clint decided not to mention the dream he'd had during his fifteen-minute nap.

"I find all of this interesting," Clint told him. "And the Count is offering me the job of headliner. If I'm even going to consider it, I have to know more."

"Who you kiddin'?" Bizzy said. "You ain't even thinkin' about it."

"Be that as it may," Clint said, "if I know somebody's doing something wrong, something that might hurt children—"

"Wow!" Bizzy said, cutting him off. "Kyra really got into your head, didn't she? Did she sleep with you?"

"No," Clint said, "and no."

"Look," Bizzy said, "I'm only talkin' to ya because Emmy asked me to. But that don't mean I'm gonna help you sabotage the Count."

"Whoa," Clint said, "who said I want to sabotage anyone?"

"I don't know what you wanna do," Bizzy said, pushing his empty plate away. "But I'm done eatin', so this conversation's over."

Bizzy stood up and left the tent. It was then Clint noticed that Emmy was also gone. The fat woman must have moved stealthily in order to get out without him noticing. Maybe she had more talents than the obvious ones—eating.

He finished his excellent steak, wondering why Kyra would send him to Bizzy. She must've known the little man wouldn't talk against the Count.

Maybe, Clint thought, he should start talking to the others he had already met and see what they had to say about the Count.

He decided to start with Smilin' Jack and see where that conversation would take them.

***

Where else was there in Freakville for the oddities to congregate, except for the two tents—the mess, and the big top?

But Jack wasn't in either one.

"Anybody seen Jack?" Clint asked, in the big top.

"He was here this mornin'," Lefty said. "Don't know where he is now."

Lefty went back to his juggling.

Clint walked across the tent to where Gordo was lifting.

"Gordo, have you seen Jack?"

Gordo put down the stone he had been lifting and looked at Clint.

"Saw him this mornin'," the big man said. "Not since. Why you want 'im?"

"I just want to ask him some questions," Clint said.

The big black man wiped the sweat from his face with a rag and said, "What questions?"

"I heard something about the Count," Clint said. "I wanted to check with Jack and see what he knew."

"We all know about the Count," Gordo said. "What did you hear?"

"That he has bad intentions," Clint said. "Evil ones, in fact."

"Ah," Gordo said, "you been talkin' to Kyra."

"That's right."

"You have to remember Kyra's a witch," Gordo said.

"And?"

"Witches lie," Gordo said. "Everybody knows that."

Chapter Twenty-Seven

"Does that include Belle?" Clint asked.

"She's a witch, isn't she?" Gordo said. "They all lie."

"I see," Clint said. "Gordo, since I have you here and, for a change, you're talking, tell me about Angus McDougal."

"Oh, the Irishman," Gordo said. "The Count's mortal enemy."

"Enemy is a strong word, isn't it?"

"He is the competition," Gordo said. "To the Count, that's the same as enemy."

"How long have you known the Count?"

"A few years," Gordo said. "I was working as a blacksmith when he found me and asked me to come here."

"A blacksmith?"

"It is my only other talent," he said.

Clint wanted to ask if strength was really a talent, but he decided not to.

"Gordo," he said, instead, "thanks for talking to me."

"I'll go back to work now," the strongman said.

"I'll leave you to it."

Clint looked around the tent before leaving, saw something he hadn't noticed before. There were women there, rehearsing. One seemed to be twisting her body into different shapes, another looked like she was meditating. He realized there were still many of the fifty or sixty oddities in Freakville he hadn't seen yet.

***

Clint didn't know where to get a drink in Freakville. He went to the mess tent, but instead of getting coffee, or standing in line for food, he went to the front of the line and asked, "Where can I get a drink?"

The woman dishing out the food stared at him, as if she couldn't hear him.

"She's deaf," the first person in line said. "What kind of drink you want? Wine? Whiskey?"

"Beer," Clint said.

"You need to talk to Curtis."

"Who's Curtis?"

"You know Bizzy?"

"Sure."

"Curtis is just a little taller than him," the skinny man said.

"Where do I find Curtis?"

The man turned and craned his neck.

"Back table," he said. "He's finishin' his meal."

"Thanks."

Clint walked to the table where a small man was eating. There were a couple of other people at the table, as well. They looked like two, normal workmen.

"Curtis?"

The little man looked up at Clint. His features were perfect, unlike Bizzy's, which were exaggerated. This oddity looked like a perfect, miniature man.

"You're Clint Adams." He had a very high voice.

"That's right."

"What can I do for you, sir?"

"I've been told you're the man to see about getting a beer."

"We do have a special place," Curtis said. "I was just finishing up here. A beer sounds good to me." He stood. "Follow me."

As he trailed after the man, he realized he had stood behind him in line for food the first time he ate there.

"See," the little man said, "the Count doesn't like his people drinking, so we do it privately."

"You keep things from the Count?" Clint asked.

"Just this," Curtis said. "Nothing else, really. But the Count pretty much believes what I tell him."

"Why's that?"

"I'm his right-hand man," Curtis said. "Or right-hand half-man." He laughed, a high pitch, scratchy sound. "I joke about my size."

"I see."

Curtis led Clint down a street he hadn't been on, yet. It seemed as deserted as many of the others, but they stopped in front of a building and Curtis knocked three times on the door. It was opened by a stocky, powerfully built man wearing an apron around his waist.

"I brought a friend for a beer," Curtis said.

"Come on in."

They entered and Clint was surprised. The interior was set up as a small saloon, complete with a bar, tables and chairs. Several men were sitting with drinks in front of them. One of them was Smilin' Jack.

"Mr. Adams." Jack said. "You found your way to our little hideaway."

"I was looking for you," Clint said, "and then I went looking for a beer and found Curtis."

"Have a seat," Jack said. "Mike, a beer for Mr. Adams."

"Comin' up," the stocky man said.

He and Curtis went to the bar. The little man had a drink while standing there. Mike brought a frothy beer to the table and set it in front of Clint.

"So the Count doesn't know about this place?" Clint said to Jack.

"He's a bit of a stickler about drinking," Jack said.

"He doesn't drink?"

"Oh, *he* does," Jack said. "He just doesn't want any of his people doing it."

"How many of you know about this place?"

"Quite a few," Jack said, "but we're all sworn to secrecy. It's sort of like a private club." The smiling man picked up his beer and raised it to Clint. "And now you're a member. Welcome!"

Chapter Twenty-Eight

"Why were you looking for me?" Jack asked.

"I had some questions I wanted to ask," Clint said. "While looking for you, I actually found Gordo in a talkative mood."

"That's rare," Jack said. "What did he have to say?"

"He answered some questions I had about the Irishman," Clint said.

"And who told you about him?"

"Belle did."

"That must mean the Count wanted you to know about him," Jack said. "He must think you knowing about McDougal will put you on his side."

"His side of what?"

"Their feud," Jack said. "They've been competing for a long time. Now they're competing to get their shows up and running first."

"I would think the Irishman would have an advantage being in Flagstaff," Clint said.

"You'd think that," Jack said, "but the Count already has some of the acts the Irishman wanted."

"So he has a leg up on McDougal."

"Two legs, if he gets you," Jack predicted. "Is he getting you? Has Belle convinced you?"

"No," Clint said, "and no. I also spoke with Kyra."

"Ah, how did you find her?" Jack asked. "Or did she find you?"

"She had Emmy introduce us."

"Kyra might be Emmy's only friend."

"Why is that?" Clint asked. "She's so sweet."

"I don't know," Jack said. "It seems to me that no one likes to be around fat people."

"With all the oddities you have here, how can fat be so bad?"

"I can't answer that," Jack said. "Hey, I like Emmy, too, but if you notice, she always eats at a table alone."

"I noticed," Clint said, "and so does she. Well, I'm glad she has at least one friend."

"And you," Jack said.

"Right, and me. I don't think Bizzy's too happy about that."

"Bizzy's not too happy about anything."

"Does he know about this little club?"

"Hell, no," Jack said. "Bizzy can't handle his liquor, at all."

"There's something else Kyra told me that I'm wondering about," Clint said.

"What's that?"

"She has this idea that the Count is evil," Clint said. "In fact, she went so far as to call him the Devil."

"You have to understand something about witches."

"Gordo told me," Clint said. "They all lie."

"That's right," Jack said, "and they have their own private reasons for what they do. Which none of us can figure out."

"Belle said that the Count owned her," Clint said.

"Belle and the Count have their own arrangement," Jack said. "He tried it with Kyra, but she wasn't having it. So he has Belle."

"Belle seems like an intelligent woman," Clint said. "Why would she let a man own her?"

"I can only think of one reason."

"And what's that?"

"He has something of hers," Jack said. "Something she can't live without."

"So as long as he has whatever that is, he can control her," Clint said.

"Right."

"And if he didn't have it, she'd be free to go and do as she pleases?"

"I guess so."

"So, do you agree with Kyra?" Clint asked. "Is the Count evil?"

"The Count is the Count," Jack said. "I ain't never seen him actually do anything I'd call evil."

"She says he wants to travel the West with his show, passing his evil on to children."

"I don't understand how Kyra could know something like that," Jack said. "Witch or no witch."

"Tell me something," Clint said. "Do Belle and Kyra get along?"

"Like cats and dogs," Jack said. "In fact, they stay away from each other. They're both witches, but they're very different."

"I find them both intelligent women," Clint said.

"There are a lot of carny and circus people who are intelligent, Mr. Adams," Jack said. "Personally, I'm from back East, and I have a law degree. What am I doing here? I'm also a freak."

"I see."

"I'm curious," Jack said. "Why are you still here, if you're not going to join the show?"

"You know," Clint said, "I've been asking myself the same question."

"If you're interested in the Irishman, maybe you should talk to him."

"You mean, go to Flagstaff?"

"Gordo and I are going tomorrow to pick up supplies," Jack said. "We generally spend the night and come back the next day. That gives us time for a drink or two and a good meal in a real restaurant."

"That all sounds good."

"And you'll find something else interesting."

"What's that?"

"No matter who goes to Flagstaff for supplies—and we take turns—Curtis goes along. When we get there, he goes off by himself, then he meets up with us the next day to come back."

"And what's Curtis' business in Flagstaff?"

"None of us know," Jack said. "Care to make a guess?"

"The Count gets information from Flagstaff, doesn't he? About the Irishman? Could be that's what Curtis is doing."

"Could be."

"You've got something else in mind," Clint said, and then he got it. "Oh, I see. You think Curtis is giving the Irishman information about what's going on here. Either that, or he's playing both ends against the middle."

"Curtis is very smart," Jack said. "It's for sure he's got something going for himself."

"Looks like I'm taking a ride to Flagstaff tomorrow," Clint said.

Chapter Twenty-Nine

The next morning Clint saddled his Tobiano and met Jack, Gordo and Curtis in front of the big top tent as they pulled the buckboard out.

"Does the Count know you're coming along?" Curtis asked.

"Do I need his permission?" Clint asked.

"I suppose not," Curtis said.

He climbed up into the buckboard without help from anyone, sat next to Jack, who was driving. Gordo was in the back.

They pulled out of Freakville with Clint riding alongside.

***

The Count was having his breakfast when Belle came in and looked at him.

"What is it?"

"I thought you'd like to know that Clint Adams went to Flagstaff with the supply wagon.

The Count stopped eating.

"Is he going to come back?" he demanded.

"Of course he is," she said. "I'm here, aren't I?"

"You're sure he's coming back?"

"Positive," Belle lied.

"You better be right, Belle."

"I'll cast a spell or two," she told him, "just to make sure."

As she left the room he muttered, "Fucking spells."

***

Clint and the oddities rode into Flagstaff, with Smilin' Jack driving the buggy to the hotel they usually stayed at. Flagstaff was a growing town, but they weren't there to see the sights.

As Jack put the brake on, he said to Clint, "We'll hit the mercantile in the morning and get all the supplies. They should have most of them ready for us. We have a standing order."

"I'll be there to help you load up," Clint said.

Curtis climbed down from the buckboard on his own and said, "I'll meet you all back here tomorrow," and off he went.

"You going to follow him?" Jack asked.

"You bet I am," Clint said.

"I'll take care of your horse," Gordo said.

"Thanks, big guy."

"He's going to lead you right to the Irishman," Jack said. "I bet I'm right."

"See you later."

"We'll wait in the hotel for you and then we'll all get something to eat when you get back."

"Deal," Clint said, and started walking after the little man before he lost him.

***

Curtis led Clint to an expensive looking hotel called The Domino House. He watched him walk through the lobby and directly up a flight of stairs to the second floor. He then hurried across the lobby himself, hoping to get upstairs in time to see what room he went into. As he reached the hall, he saw Curtis enter and close the door behind him. Clint went to the door and saw the number "10" on it. Satisfied, he went to check with the front desk.

"Room ten?" the clerk said, pocketing the dollar Clint had given him. "Yes, sir, that's Mr. McDougal's room. He's one of our permanent guests."

"Permanent?"

"Well, that is," the clerk said, "he's not going day-to-day. See, he doesn't know when he's going to leave, so the manager gave him a special rate."

"Do you know who the little man is who visits him?"

"No, sir," the clerk said, "just that he comes here a couple of times a month."

"Thank you."

Clint went into the hotel dining room. It was fairly empty, so he was able to get a table from which he'd be able to watch the lobby. He had a cup of coffee and waited to see Curtis leave.

Chapter Thirty

After about thirty-five minutes Clint saw Curtis go out the front door of the hotel. He waited until the count of ten, then paid for his coffee and went up the stairs to room ten and knocked.

"Didja forget somethin', lad," a tall, red-haired man said, as he opened the door. He was looking down, but when he realized it wasn't Curtis who knocked, he looked up again. "Sorry," he said, "I was expectin' someone a wee bit smaller."

"Mr. McDougal?"

"That's me, McDougal."

"Otherwise known as the Irishman?"

"I'm an Irishman, yes," McDougal said, slowly.

"My name's Clint Adams."

McDougal looked surprised.

"Curtis told me you'd probably be visitin' me, he just didn't say how soon. Come in, lad, come in."

McDougal backed away from the door to allow Clint to enter and close the door behind him.

"I've a bottle of Irish whiskey here," McDougal said. "Would you like some?"

"No, thanks," Clint said. "Why did Curtis say I'd be coming to see you?"

"He said the Count was tryin' to sign you up, but you weren't goin' for it. So he figured maybe you'd be comin' here for a better deal." The man smiled. "I can make you a better deal, all right." McDougal was in his forties, wearing a green three-piece suit. On the bed was a green derby hat.

"I'm not looking for a deal," Clint told the man. "But I am looking for some information."

"About what?" McDougal sat down in one of the armchairs. "You wanna sit?"

"I won't be here that long," Clint said. "Tell me what you know about the Count."

"What do you wanna know?"

"Well, for starters, do you know his real name?"

"I know a few names he's used over the years," McDougal said. "Don't know which one's his real one."

"How do you know him?" Clint asked. "I heard you and he have been competing for a long time."

"Ever since we ended our partnership."

"You were partners?" Clint asked surprised.

"Yup," McDougal said. "Had ourselves a little side show. Wasn't much, just a few freaks. But he wanted to go his own way and build himself somethin' bigger."

"How many years ago was that?"

"Probably 'bout twelve, fifteen maybe."

"And he's still trying?"

"Oh, he's had a show or two, but nothin' that lasted."

"And you?"

"Same thing," the Irishman said. "I'm still tryin' to build myself up. You know, with you I could build somethin' real big."

"That's what the Count thinks," Clint said. "But I'm not going to be his headliner, or yours."

"Then I guess I'll just have to go with what I got," McDougal said.

"What about Curtis?" Clint asked. "Is he working for both of you?"

"Curtis keeps me informed," McDougal said.

"For a fee."

"Sure. Everythin's for a fee."

"And you don't think he's doing the same thing to you, telling the Count what you've got going?"

"Sure he is," McDougal said, "but I don't tell him everythin'."

"You got any witches in your show?"

"I don't believe in witches," McDougal said, "but I've got some fortune tellers."

"One of the Count's witches told me she thinks he's evil," Clint said. "What do you think?"

"If he's evil, it's somethin' that happened to him over the years," McDougal said. "I know he's sent a man or two here to sabotage my show. Started a fire one time, destroyed a bunch of my tents."

"And what about you?" Clint asked. "What've you done to him?"

"Nothin' that bad," McDougal said. "I snatched away a few of his acts by offerin' more money. That's the way to really hurt him."

"And how long is this . . . this feud going to go on?" Clint asked.

"Feud?" McDougal scratched his jaw. "Yeah, I guess you could call it a feud. And I guess it'll go on as long as we both live." The Irishman stood up, picked up his hat. "Seems to me if you ain't gonna sign with him, or me, you ought to just move on."

"I'm thinking the same thing," Clint said, "but I promised to help bring back their supplies. After that, maybe . . ."

"Well, I'm goin' out for some supper," the man in green said. "You wanna come along?"

"No thanks," Clint said. "I'm meeting the men I rode in with for supper."

"Then I guess I'll just walk out with ya, Mr. Adams."

Chapter Thirty-One

Clint met Jack and Gordo at the hotel. He realized the place didn't have a name out front.

"There's a small cafe down the street. It's got pretty good food," Jack said.

"And they don't mind freaks," Gordo said.

"Okay, fellas," Clint said, "lead the way."

They walked down the street to the café and secured a back table. It was a busy place, with two waiters working the floor.

"You're back," the older waiter said. "Welcome. What'll ya have?"

"The thickest steak you have," Gordo said.

"And you fellas?"

"The same for me," Clint said.

"Beef stew for me," Jack said. "And three beers."

"Comin' up," the waiter said.

"So," Jack said, "where did Curtis lead you?"

"Like you said," Clint replied, "right to the Irish-man."

"What'd you do?"

"I had a talk with him."

"Did he try to recruit you?"

"He did," Clint said. "I told him I wasn't interested."

"How'd he take it?"

"Fine, since he also knew I wasn't going to join the Count. But it sure looks to me like Curtis is playing both sides."

"Curtis is smart," Gordo said.

"That's true," Jack said. "He's just makin' what he can in case neither show starts up."

"That's one way of looking at it," Clint said. "I think once I help you get your supplies back to Freakville it'll be time for me to be on my way."

"Too bad," Jack said. "I was looking forward to more poker lessons."

"I might have time for one more game," Clint said.

"Maybe the three of us could play tonight, in one of our rooms," Jack said, "Gordo?"

"I like poker," Gordo said.

"That'd be a good way to pass the time," Clint said. "What about Curtis? Does he play?"

"Naw, never has," Jack said. "Besides, we won't see him til tomorrow. I think he's got a woman in town."

"Curtis has a girlfriend," Gordo said.

The waiter came with their plates and beers, set them all down, including a basket of fresh rolls. All three men devoured their meals with gusto, then ordered pie for dessert. Gordo had rhubarb, Clint's least favorite. The strong man attacked it like a mule at a salt lick.

"I'm curious about these little men," Clint admitted. "Bizzy is married to Emmy, and you say Curtis has a girlfriend. Do they, uh . . ."

"They're just like other men," Jack said. "They like bein' with women, no matter what size."

"But Bizzy and Emmy?" Clint asked.

"I know," Jack said, "we all wonder about that."

"I like Emmy," Gordo said.

"Why don't you ever sit with her when she eats?" Clint asked.

"Bizzy threatened me," Gordo said. "He's a mean little man."

"He scares you?" Clint asked.

"He scares lots of people," Jack said.

"But Gordo," Clint said, "you could crush him, easily."

"I wouldn't touch him," Gordo said, and then repeated, "He's mean."

"I think he's just jealous," Clint said. "He warned me off, too."

"Jealous," Gordo said, "and mean."

***

They went back to the oddly unnamed hotel after supper, to the room Jack and Gordo were sharing. Jack produced a deck of cards, and they played some low stakes poker with matchsticks.

Clint showed them the proper way to bet, and how to identify other player's "tells."

It was late when they quit, and Clint walked down the hall to his own room. He stopped just outside because he smelled something. He opened the door slowly with his left hand, his right hand down by his gun.

"Where've you been?" Kyra asked. "I've been waiting for hours."

He closed the door. She was sitting on the bed with her legs crossed, wearing a long blue dress that covered her from neck to ankles.

"You're not surprised to see me," she said.

"I smelled you in the hall," he said. "How'd you get here?"

"I'm a witch," she reminded him. "I have ways of getting places."

"And how did you know I'd be here?"

"Same answer," she said. "I have ways."

"Okay, then why are you here?"

"Now," she said, "that's a question I can answer. Do you have anything to drink?"

"No," he said. "For that we need to go downstairs."

She stood up. "That suits me."

Chapter Thirty-Two

The hotel had a small saloon just off the lobby. At this time of night, it was empty but still open. It seemed to cater only to hotel guests.

They took a table in the back and Clint asked the bartender for a beer.

"And for the lady?" the man asked.

"Just a glass of red wine, if you have it," Kyra said.

"Of course."

"It's thirsty work," she said, "just sitting in your room, waiting for you. Where were you, anyway?"

"Just down the hall, in Jack and Gordo's room," he said.

The bartender came with their drinks and set them down gently.

"Thanks," Clint said.

Kyra sipped her red wine gratefully. Clint did the same with his beer.

"Now what's this about?" he asked. "What brings you to Flagstaff? Don't tell me you're here to see the Irishman?"

"Of course not," she said. "He's just as bad as the Count."

"So you're not here to see him," Clint said.

"No, silly," she said. "I'm here to see you."

"About what?"

"I told you," she said. "You have to stop the Count."

"Because he's evil."

"Exactly."

"You know, I spoke with McDougal, the Irishman," he said. "He and the Count used to be partners, and he doesn't think he's evil."

"That's because evil doesn't necessarily recognize evil," she explained.

"So you're saying the Irishman is also evil."

"Of course."

"Why of course?"

"You see the rabble they choose to consort with," she said.

"Aren't you part of that rabble?"

"Please," she said, "I'm nothing like Belle and all those other freaks. I'm trying to save people from their evil."

"As a witch," he said, "don't you have the power to do that? Why do you need me?"

"I can only do so much," she said. "I need you to actually stop them."

"I don't think that's going to be up to me," he said. "My plan when I get back to Freakville is to pack up and move on."

"That's your plan now," she said. "It will change."

"Will it?" he asked. "Because of your witchcraft."

"No," she said, "because of your good heart. You are a man who can't walk away from people in need."

"What makes you say that?" he asked. "You know my reputation."

"The reputation of a man seldom describes the real man," she said.

He couldn't argue with that. It was exactly how he felt. But then, was that why she was saying it?

"You're not some kind of mind reader, are you?" he asked.

"No," she said, "that's a totally different talent. Much like communing with the dead. I can't do that, either." She finished her wine and said, "I'm just a simple witch."

She stood up, even though he was only half finished with his beer.

"Shall we go to your room?" she said. "I'm rather tired."

"You plan to sleep in my room?"

"Well, of course," she said. "I'm only here for the one night, and I couldn't get a room. You wouldn't want me to sleep in the street, or a barn, would you?"

"No," he said, also standing, "we wouldn't want that."

They left the saloon and went to his room.

***

Curtis got back to the hotel in time to see Clint and Kyra in the lobby. He stayed out of sight and watched them go up the stairs together.

After his meeting with the Irishman—where he both gave and received information—he went to visit a woman named Nicole Daniels. She was a wealthy, attractive widow in her early forties, who he knew had many lovers. For some reason she was fascinated by the juxtaposition of his diminutive size with his large penis. He had spent the day, and most of the evening in bed with her, and then taken his leave, feeling pleasantly fatigued. After that he had gone for a late supper at a restaurant he liked, before returning to the hotel.

Seeing Kyra in Flagstaff was a surprise to him. Since her arrival in Freakville she had rarely left. He prided himself in knowing the idiosyncrasies of every freak in town. Why, then, had she decided to travel to Flagstaff?

And how had she gotten there? She didn't own a horse or a buggy, and there were none to be had in Freakville, save the buckboard he and the others had come in on.

He decided to broach the subject with the Gunsmith the next morning. Since he brought information back-and-forth between the Irishman and the Count, he didn't like being uninformed.

Chapter Thirty-Three

As they entered his room he said, "You can have the bed. I'll sleep in that chair."

"I have a better idea," she said.

"What's that?"

He looked at her, and she dropped her dress to the floor, revealing her naked body. She was long and sleek, with small, perfect breasts and slender hips. Her nipples were pink and already hard. Her aroma suddenly filled the room and made him dizzy.

"Was that your plan when you came here?" he asked. "Seduce me and get me to do what you want?"

"Why no," she said, "I was just looking at this as a nice way to relax so I can fall asleep." She ran her hands over her body. "Do you mind?"

"Well," he said, "not when you put it that way."

She pulled the blanket down off the bed as he removed his gunbelt and hung it on the bedpost.

"I suppose that's necessary for a man with your reputation," she said.

"Always," he said.

"Very well," she said. "Get your clothes off and join me in bed."

She didn't have to ask—or tell him twice. When he was naked, he got in bed with her, gathered her close so their bodies were pressed tightly together, and kissed her. The heady scent of her increased. He actually felt that his senses were being affected. Both touch and smell seemed very acute, and the taste of her mouth was intoxicating.

Then she slid her mouth from his and began to kiss his neck, and shoulders, and chest and the sensation of her lips on him actually made him shudder. He thought briefly of her claim to be a witch, but decided he was being affected by her allure as a woman, not her power as a witch.

She kissed her way down his body until her face was pressed to his hard cock. Then, when she took him lovingly into her mouth, he started to feel like he was in a dream. She sucked him until he could hold back no more. When he exploded and felt as if his mind was swirling . . .

***

Had it been a dream?

When he woke, he had memories of the things they had done all night. At one point he remembered taking her from behind, and the sound of her laughter as he pounded away at her until he climaxed . . . but now she was gone.

He sat up in bed and looked around. The sun was streaming in through the window, so it was morning, but there was no sign of her in the room, except for her scent, which lingered in his nostrils. Oddly, though, when he sniffed the sheets, they didn't smell of her. The aroma only seemed to be in his nose.

He got to his feet and found that he was unsteady. His legs were weak, and he was slightly dizzy. He sat back down waiting for the dizziness to pass. After a few moments he stood, washed, and dressed. He strapped on his gun, grabbed his rifle and saddlebags and left the room to meet Jack and Gordo downstairs.

"You look like you had a hell of a night," Jack said, as he joined them in the lobby.

"I might have had a wild dream," he said.

"Tell us about it over breakfast," Jack said. "Gordo is starving."

The big black man nodded, and Clint said, "You know what? So am I."

***

He told them that he had seen Kyra the night before.

"She was in my room when I got there," Clint said. "Then we went down and had a drink, before going back to my room for the night."

"That must've been a dream," Jack said. "Kyra would have no way of getting here."

"There must be a horse or a buggy in Freakville she could've used."

"We only have the one horse and buckboard that we came in on," Jack said.

"What about the wagon Emmy and Bizzy were in when I met them?"

"That piece of junk would never make it here," Jack said. "Besides, we have the only horse."

"Well," Clint said, "she was here." He could still smell her.

"Kyra never leaves town," Gordo said. "She hardly ever leaves her house."

"It had to be a dream," Jack said. "What did she say?"

"All that talk about evil," Clint said. "That the Count is evil, and so is the Irishman, and if they're allowed to put their shows on the road, they'll be spreading that evil."

"Wow," Jack said, "that was some dream. If there's so much evil, why is she even with us?"

"She's not," Gordo said. "Kyra lives in Freakville, but she's not *with* us. She's on her own."

Jack looked at Gordo, then back at Clint again.

"Still," he said, "had to be a dream."

Chapter Thirty-Four

Clint didn't like the idea that he might not be able to tell reality from fantasy. He was going to have to ask a lot of questions when they got back to Freakville. For now, he'd concentrate on loading up the supplies so they could leave Flagstaff.

When they reached the mercantile, their order was ready to be loaded. Clint and Gordo started, while Jack went in to purchase a few odd items that weren't on the regular order list. Halfway through the loading, Curtis arrived, looking neat and well-groomed. He stood off to the side and didn't help, at all.

When Clint and Gordo finished, they waited while Jack came back out and tossed his few items onto the buckboard.

"Are we ready to go?" Jack asked.

They had tied Clint's Tobiano to the back of the buckboard, so he untied it and mounted up as the other three climbed onto the wagon—Jack and Curtis on the seat, and Gordo on the bed with the supplies.

"I'm ready to go," Clint said.

"Me, too," Gordo echoed.

Jack picked up the reins, shook them at the horse, and they were on their way. Clint wondered why, in the entire town of 50 or 60 people, there was only one horse in Freakville. The trip back would've been easier with a team pulling.

He also couldn't help thinking about Kyra during the ride back . . .

***

They left early enough so that they'd be able to make the trip by nightfall, and not have to camp for the night. It was just getting dark when they rode back into town, taking the buckboard right to the big top and inside.

As soon as they got into the tent, Curtis jumped down from the buckboard and was gone. Clint assumed the little man was going directly to the Count to report in.

"Do you need help unloading?" Clint asked.

"No," Jack said, "we've got plenty of men for that."

"Want me to see to your horse?" Gordo asked.

He was very good with the Tobiano, so Clint said, "Thanks, Gordo."

He left the tent and headed right for Kyra's house. He wanted to get this straight in his head, once and for all.

***

When he got to Kyra's house, he knocked and waited. It was possible she wasn't back from Flagstaff, yet.

But she answered the door and stared at him oddly. "Yes?"

"How did you get back here so fast?" he asked.

"I'm sorry," she said. "Back from where?"

"Can I come in?"

"Of course." She backed away to allow him to enter.

"Do you have anything to drink?" he asked. "I just got back from Flagstaff."

"You must be exhausted," she said. "Come and sit, I'll give you something to eat and drink."

She had a large pot hanging in the fireplace, and a smaller one next to it.

"I have stew and tea," she said. "Is that all right?"

"It sounds fine."

The table and chairs she had were made of thick wood, very sturdy. He sat and waited, wondering how to approach the subject with her.

"I was about to have supper myself," she said, putting two bowls on the table, "so we'll eat together and you can tell me what's on your mind."

She set two cups of tea down and sat across from him.

"You never eat in the mess tent with the others?" he asked.

"No," she said, "usually I prefer to eat alone. Besides, if I go there, they all stare."

"*They* stare at *you*?" he said.

"Yes, I know," she said. "They're all freaks, but they consider me odd."

"Even Emmy?"

She smiled.

"Emmy is sweet," Kyra said. "She's probably my only friend in town. How's the stew?"

He tasted it.

"It's very good. Thank you."

"Now then," she said, just before putting a spoonful into her mouth, "what brings you here, Mr. Adams?"

"Don't you think that after spending last night together you could call me Clint?"

"I'm sorry," she said. "Spending last night together?"

"That's right."

She put her spoon down.

"I think perhaps you ought to tell me exactly what you think happened last night," she told him.

Chapter Thirty-Five

Kyra listened intently as Clint told her what had happened between them in Flagstaff. They continued to eat while he spoke and were finished by the time he was done.

"All right," she said, "now it's your turn to listen. I didn't leave this house yesterday; I haven't been to Flagstaff; I was never in your room; and we most certainly didn't spend the night together."

"So you're telling me . . . what are you telling me?" he asked. "That I dreamed it?"

"I guess so," she said. "I suppose I should be flattered."

Clint breathed in and caught her scent, the same aroma from the night before. But he could also have been remembering it from the first time they met.

"If it wasn't a dream," she said, "do you think I flew to Flagstaff on my broom?"

"I don't know what I think," Clint said, smiling, "but it's not that."

"Would you like some more to eat?" she asked.

"No, thanks," he said. "I think I've taken up enough of your time with my . . . dream."

She walked him to the door.

"There's something else," she said.

"What's that?"

"You said I had a glass of red wine."

"That's right."

"I don't drink," she said, "*ever*."

"Then I'm sorry I bothered you."

"Have you decided what you're going to do about the Count?" she asked.

"Not yet," he said. "I'll let you know."

"I'll be here," she said.

He stepped outside and she closed the door behind him. He wasn't convinced that what he had experienced was a dream. It was possible she was lying to him, to make the experience seem like it was something . . . magical. But there was no point in calling her a liar to her face. Not yet, anyway.

***

After Clint left her house Kyra closed the door, walked back to the kitchen area, got a bottle of red wine from her cupboard and poured herself a glass, with a smile.

Clint went looking for Emmy, figuring she was the only one to talk to about Kyra. Though he didn't find her in the mess tent, he did find Gordo there, eating.

"Hey Gordo, Emmy and Bizzy live in the hotel, right?"

"Yeah." Gordo asked.

"Do you know which room?"

"No, I never been there."

"Thanks," Clint said. "I'll find it."

Gordo reached out and grabbed Clint's left wrist in a tight grip.

"You want some advice?"

"Sure."

"Don't let Bizzy catch you alone in their room with Emmy," the big man said. "He's mean. Little people are mean."

"Thanks for the advice."

Gordo nodded, released Clint's wrist and went back to his meal.

***

When Clint got to the hotel, he knew there'd be nobody to ask. He decided to just knock on doors until he found the right room. He knocked twice before somebody told him what room they were in. It happened to be right down the hall from his. He stopped in front of the door, was about to knock when he thought he heard something from inside. It sounded like grunting and groaning, and then he thought he heard the sound of a slap—certainly flesh-on-flesh. He decided to knock and apologize later if he was interrupting.

He heard footsteps to the door, and then it swung open. Bizzy stood in the doorway, naked as a jaybird, with a huge erection. On the bed was Emmy, with acres and acres of naked flesh on display. When she saw Clint, she hurriedly covered herself with a sheet.

"We're a little busy right now, Adams," Bizzy snapped.

"Sorry," Clint said, "I just wanted to talk to Emmy about something."

"It'll have to wait until we're finished," the little man said.

Clint, trying to look away from the disconcerting sight of the little man's large, enraged cock, said, "Sure, okay, sorry to bother you."

Bizzy slammed the door. In scant moments, Clint heard the grunting and groaning again, and quickly moved away from the door.

Chapter Thirty-Six

Clint went to his own room and sat on the bed. He didn't know if he felt embarrassed, or if he was simply . . . aghast. He couldn't get the image of Bizzy out of his mind. He waited fifteen minutes and was about to leave his room when there was a knock at the door. When he opened it, Emmy was standing there, looking embarrassed. She was holding her robe closed.

"I'm sorry," she said, "I didn't want you to see—"

"Where's Bizzy?" Clint asked, looking into the hall.

"He's asleep," she said. "He always falls asleep right after we . . ."

"Come on in," he said.

She entered the room, took the time to tie the robe at her waist, so that it remained closed without her holding it.

"What'll happen if he catches you here?" Clint asked.

"He won't," she said. "When he—when we—he'll sleep all night now."

"I'm sorry," he said, "I don't have anything to offer you to drink."

"That's all right," she said. "What did you want to see me about?"

"Kyra," he said. "I wanted to talk to you about Kyra."

"What about her?"

"What I'm about to tell you may sound weird, but I need your opinion."

"All right." She sat on the bed to listen.

He told her what he thought had happened in Flagstaff between himself and Kyra. She listened intently and didn't say a word until he was finished.

"So?" he said, "what do you think?"

"What do you want me to tell you?" she asked.

"I've been told that all witches lie," he said. "Is Kyra lying to me?"

"I don't know," she said. "I can tell you that she hasn't left town since she first arrived months ago. I can say I don't know how she would have got to Flagstaff and back so quickly."

"Well," he said, "if she really is a witch . . ."

"You mean the flying on a broom kind?" she asked. "I don't think so."

"Then do you think I dreamed the whole thing?"

"It's possible—"

"But it was so real," he said. "I could smell her on me the next morning." He didn't tell Emmy that he couldn't smell Kyra on the bed sheets.

"I don't know what else I can tell you, Clint," Emmy said. "I've found Kyra to always be truthful with me. But if you talk to anyone else around here, they all have the same opinion. They're afraid of her."

Clint sat in a chair and shook his head.

"I can't believe it was a dream," he said. "Is it true there's only one horse in town, to pull the buckboard and your wagon?"

"Yes, that's all," she said. "We had another, but it was old and just . . . died, one day."

"Why doesn't the Count get another one?"

"He's real careful with his money," she said. "That's why he only sends someone to Flagstaff for supplies about twice a month."

"Who else can I talk to about Kyra?" he asked. "Belle?"

"Belle and Kyra are opposites," she said. "Neither one will have anythin' good to say about the other one."

"The Count, then?"

"I don't really know what his relationship is with Kyra," Emmy admitted.

"What about Curtis?"

For a moment she shivered, then asked, "What about him?"

"What do you know about him?"

"He's a horrible little man," she said. "Oh, I know what you're thinkin' that Bizzy's horrible, but he's not. Bizzy is ornery, but Curtis . . . he's a bad man. If there's evil in this camp, it's Curtis."

"I wondered about that," Clint said. "I followed him in Flagstaff, and he went right to the Irishman."

"I thought he might be doin' that," she said.

"Do you think the Count knows?"

"Probably," Emmy said.

"I thought Curtis was playing both ends," Clint said, "but maybe it's the Irishman and the Count who are using Curtis."

"I don't know about that," she said. "If you listen to Bizzy, I'm not a smart woman, but I think those three all have their own plan."

"If Bizzy thinks of you that way, why stay with him, Emmy?" Clint asked.

"We're married," she said. "He loves me. And what other man would have me?"

"A man would be a fool not to want a woman like you, Emmy," he said.

She blushed and said, "I've gotta get back." She stood up. "I hope I was helpful."

"Very helpful," he said. "Thanks for coming down the hall."

"Sure."

He opened the door for her and watched her walk back down the hall to her own room before closing it.

Chapter Thirty-Seven

Clint tried to put Kyra out of his mind and go to sleep, but he kept jerking awake, thinking he was seeing her in his room, smiling at him. Once he thought he saw her naked, but it really was a dream that time.

He woke in a sweat with the sun on his face, the unpleasant feel of damp sheets beneath him. He got up, washed himself off as best he could with the water in the basin, and went downstairs for breakfast.

He got to the mess tent before seven a.m., so there weren't many of the freaks and oddities there. But, strangely enough, one who was eating at a table alone was Curtis. He collected a plate of ham-and-eggs from the deaf woman who served, got himself a cup of coffee and carried them to the little man's table.

"Mind if I join you?"

"Yes," Curtis said, "I do, but you probably will, anyway."

"You're right about that," Clint said, sitting across from him.

"Did you enjoy following me in Flagstaff?" Curtis asked.

"It was very informative."

"Were you behind me the whole time?"

"Just until you finished with the Irishman," Clint said. "Then I went in and spoke with him."

That gave Curtis some relief, that Clint Adams didn't follow him to his lady friend's house. She didn't want anyone to know she was dallying with a little man. But she loved it when he took her from behind . . .

Curtis brought his mind back to the present.

"How did you two get along?" he asked Clint.

"Just fine," Clint said. "He told me he knew you were probably playing him and the Count against each other. He thinks you're smart that way."

Curtis didn't say anything.

"Is he right?" Clint asked. "Are you that smart?"

"What do you think?" Curtis asked.

"That they both think they're using you," Clint said, "but in reality, you're using them."

"You're giving me a lot of credit."

"Come on, tell me the truth," Clint said. "Do you think one of these shows is going to make it?"

"I don't really care," Curtis said, "as long as I get what I want."

"And what's that?"

"It's a private matter."

"I think you know everything that goes on in both camps," Clint said. "What can you tell me about Kyra?"

Curtis looked up from his plate and stared Clint in the eyes.

"What do you want to know about Kyra?"

"How do you get along with her?" Clint asked.

"I don't."

"Do you believe she's really a witch?"

"Why not?"

"Can you tell me how she could get to Flagstaff and back without a horse?"

"A broom?"

"Come on, Curtis," Clint said. "Is there another horse in Freakville?"

"Not that I know of," the little man said.

"Do you get along with anyone in town?" Clint asked.

"Who did you have in mind?"

"Well, Bizzy, I guess."

Curtis froze.

"Why would I get along with Bizzy?"

"I guess because you're . . . the same?"

Curtis suddenly got red in the face.

"Bizzy and I are nothing alike," he hissed. "He's a malformed dwarf. I am a perfectly formed, but small man."

"A midget then?"

"We don't like that word," Curtis said getting up.

"I'm sorry," Clint said. "I thought a dwarf and a midget were the same."

"That's because you're an ignorant man!" Curtis snapped and stormed out of the tent.

"What did you do to him?"

Clint looked up, saw Smilin' Jack approaching with a plate.

"I called him a midget."

Jack sat in the chair Curtis had just vacated.

"Ooh," he said, "the little people don't like that. They barely tolerate dwarf."

"Curtis said he's not a dwarf."

"He's a proportionate dwarf," Jack said. "Their arms and legs are shorter, but perfectly formed."

"And Bizzy?"

"Ah, he's a disproportionate dwarf," Jack replied. "His limbs are deformed, his head's big—poor guy, so are his ears and nose. So they're both little people, but very different."

"That's interesting," Clint said. "And is Bizzy so ornery because of his . . . deformities?"

"Oh," Jack said, "I think Bizzy was just born ornery, before he even realized he was deformed."

Chapter Thirty-Eight

"Jack," Clint said, "what are you doing here? You don't seem to fit in with these . . . people."

"Are you kiddin'?" Jack asked. "You see my face. I can't get this ridiculous smile to go away. Something in my face is frozen. When I was a kid, my parents took me to a dozen doctors. None of them could do a thing. Believe me, Clint, I might be *more* of a freak than a lot of these others."

"Are you comfortable here?"

"More than I have been in any other place," Jack said. "These folks accept me. And an amazing number of them are well-adjusted despite their . . . oddities."

"Maybe that's why Bizzy and Curtis stand out as . . . ornery, scary, whatever."

"Yeah," Jack said, "nobody could ever accuse those two of being well-adjusted."

"Obviously not."

"So are you gonna do it?" Jack asked.

"Do what?"

"You said when you got back here you were gonna pull out," Jack reminded him.

"Yeah, I did say that," Clint said. "But this thing with Kyra's changed my mind."

"She's in your head, isn't she?"

"My head," Clint said, "my dreams . . ."

"She's put a spell on you."

"I'd believe that if I believed in witches," Clint said.

"What else could it be?"

"You said it yourself," Clint replied. "She's in my head. I just have to get her out."

"How?"

"Maybe by finding out what the Count is really up to," Clint said.

"How do you intend to do that?"

"It might be a good start to find out his real name," Clint said, "and who he really is."

"Good luck with that," Jack said. "Everybody here just knows him as the Count."

"Do you know where he was just before he came here?" Clint asked.

"I don't," Jack said, "but I know somebody who might."

"Belle?" Clint asked.

Jack nodded.

"She can't be living in his house without finding out certain things," Jack said. "It'd be worth askin' her."

"You'd think so, wouldn't you?" Clint stood up. "Thanks, Jack."

"If you're stayin' around, maybe we could play some poker."

"Sure," Clint said. "Set it up."

He left the tent.

***

He wanted to talk with Belle but didn't want the Count to know. That meant he couldn't go to the Count's house and knock on the door. He decided to watch the house and wait for one of them to leave. If it was Belle, he could follow her and talk to her. If it was him, he could knock on the door.

He assumed the one who would leave the house would be the Count. After all, he had business to attend to. It took a little over an hour, but the front door finally opened, and the Count came out. Clint gave him time to get some distance away, then crossed over and knocked on the door.

"Clint!" Belle said in surprise, when she answered the door. "The Count just left."

"I know," Clint said. "I was watching and waiting. I want to talk to you."

"Come in," she said. "He'll be away most of the morning."

"Good."

He entered and they went into the sitting room.

"Can I offer you something? Coffee? A drink?"

"Just some conversation, for now," he said.

"Then we'd better sit."

She sat on the sofa, and he chose one of the arm-chairs.

"What's on your mind?" she asked.

"Kyra."

"Oh." She looked disappointed. "Why her?"

"She told me she thinks the Count is evil, and if his show gets on the road, he'll spread it."

"She said that?"

"Yes," he said. "Belle, do you know where the Count was before he came here?"

"I have an idea," she admitted.

"Where?"

"New York."

"What was he doing there?"

"He's never said," she told him, "but I found a letter one day when he was out."

"From who?"

"Not from," she said, "to. It was a letter he wrote to P.T. Barnum."

"What did it say?"

"He wanted to join up with Barnum," she said, "be partners."

"Did Barnum answer?"

"I'm assuming he never sent the letter but went to New York to see him."

"Obviously, it didn't go well. They're not partners."

"No, they're not."

"P.T. Barnum," Clint said.

"Did you know him?"

"I did, a while back," Clint said. "Haven't seen him in years."

"Are you surprised he turned the Count down?" Belle asked.

"No," Clint said, "not at all."

"I don't know what I can say to help you," Belle said.

Clint considered confiding in Belle about his time in Flagstaff but decided he should keep that part to himself.

"Can I do anything else?" she asked.

"I think so," he said. "Can you find that letter?"

"Probably," she said, "but not right now. It's not where it was the first time I found it."

"Why would he keep it after not sending it?" Clint wondered. "Why not throw it away?"

"I don't know," she said. "Could be he tortures himself with it. Being turned down by the great P.T. Barnum couldn't have been pleasant."

"I guess not. See if you can find it for me, will you?"

"Yes, but why do you want it?"

"I'm assuming," Clint said, "he would've signed it with his real name."

Chapter Thirty-Nine

Clint left the house, glad that Belle hadn't made any amorous advances. He wouldn't have been comfortable with that in the Count's house.

She told him she would come and tell him when she found the letter. She walked him to the door, but before leaving he asked her another question.

"Are you usually here when Curtis comes to see the Count?" he asked.

"That's odd," she said.

"Why?"

"When I *am* here, and Curtis comes, the Count tells me to take a walk."

"So you've never heard their conversations?" Clint asked.

"No," she said, "Curtis would usually say very little while I was in the house."

"And when you saw them together," Clint said, "who do you think was in charge?"

"What?" she asked. "Well, the Count—"

"Are you sure?" Clint asked. "Curtis is a pretty forceful little guy, isn't he?"

"Yes, but . . . the Count is always in charge."

"Okay, Belle," Clint said. "Thanks."

When he left the house, he was at a loss as to where to go or who to talk to next. He wondered if he should just confront the Count and ask him about Kyra's claims, or about his relationships with the Irishman and with Curtis. Maybe even mention Barnum and see how he reacted.

He went to the big top tent where most of the rehearsals took place. When he got there, only a few performers were rehearsing, and the Count wasn't there. Neither was Johnny Sharp, who he hadn't even seen since the day they shot together.

He observed a knife thrower as he hurled knives at a young woman who never flinched; watched another man pound nails into a board using his head; and admired the agility of several young men, who ran and tumbled and jumped. But none of the people he had spent time with—Jack, Gordo, Lefty—were there, yet.

He decided to simply take a walk through town and see who he ran into. As he walked past the old City Hall building, wondering if he should go inside or not, he saw another little man come out the front door and head off down the street, as if he had a special destination in mind. He decided to follow him, just for something to do.

He hadn't seen this little man before. He seemed to resemble Curtis more than Bizzy, walked with purposeful strides, not the limping steps Bizzy took on his stumpy legs.

Clint assumed this little man worked specifically for the Count, since he had come out of the City Hall building. Perhaps he was on an errand for the Count that might tell him something.

When they came to the edge of town and Clint heard the shots, he suddenly knew where the little man was headed. They eventually reached the makeshift shooting gallery Johnny Sharp used for his practice. Sharp was shooting bottles and cans again, as he had with Clint.

As the small man approached, Clint hid himself close enough to hear their conversation.

"Whataya want, Bobo?" Sharp asked

"The Count wants ta see you," the little man's high voice carried well.

"About what?"

"He didn't tell me that," Bobo said.

"Tell 'im I'll be there as soon as I'm finished here," Sharp said.

"He wants ya now," Bobo pressed.

Sharp turned and glared at the smaller man.

"Tell 'im!"

"Yeah, okay," Bobo said.

Clint ducked behind a thick tree as the little man went by, then stepped out to approach Sharp.

"What do *you* want?" Sharp asked. "To make a fool out of me again?"

"Just to talk, Johnny," Clint said. "Just to talk."

Chapter Forty

"Why don't you reload," Clint suggested.

"Why? You want to shoot with me again?"

"No, I told you," Clint said. "I just want to talk. But if you're going to wear a gun, it should always be loaded."

Sharp took the gun from his holster, ejected the spent shells, reloaded and holstered it, again.

"There, happy?"

"Very."

"Look," Sharp said, "I have to get back."

"I know, the Count wants you," Clint said. "I'll walk with you."

"Suit yourself."

They started to walk back.

"What's on your mind?"

"Your boss," Clint said. "And what he's after."

"Whataya mean?" Sharp asked. "He's tryin' to put together a show."

"Yeah, but why?"

"What do you mean?"

"I'm wondering what his angle is."

"I don't understand," Sharp said. "He wants to put on a show. That's all I know."

"Kyra thinks he wants more than just a show," Clint said. "She thinks he's got some bad intentions."

"You've talked to Kyra?" Sharp sounded surprised.

"A couple of times," Clint said.

"Kyra never talks to anybody but Emmy," he said.

"Well, she wanted to talk to me about the Count," Clint said.

"What does she want you to do?"

"She wants me to stop him."

Sharp stopped walking and looked at Clint.

"You mean, kill 'im?"

"No," Clint said, "she didn't say that. Not in so many words, anyway."

"But ain't that what you do?" Sharp asked. "Kill people?"

"I only kill people who are trying to kill me," Clint said.

They started walking again.

"I thought you were a gun for hire," the younger man said.

"No," Clint said. "Never have been and never will be. Is that what you want to be?"

"God, no!" Sharp said. "I just want to be the best shot in the world."

"Well," Clint said, "you're talented and you're young. You've got plenty of time ahead of you. You'll probably make it."

"You really think so?"

"I think you have a chance," Clint said.

"But . . . I didn't beat you."

"One day you might," Clint said. "One day you might."

***

Clint walked the young man all the way to the City Hall building, where they stopped.

"Whatever he wants with you," Clint said, "see if you can find out his ulterior motives for putting on this show."

"His what?"

"His plans," Clint said. "See if he has any plans, other than just doing a show."

"How do I do that?"

"Well," Clint said, "the easiest way would be to just ask him."

"I—I don't know if I can do that," Sharp said. "I mean, question him like that. He's the Count."

"Just see what happens," Clint said.

Sharp still had a dubious look on his face when he entered the building.

***

After leaving Johnny Sharp, Bobo went and delivered his other messages, so that three men eventually appeared in front of the Count at the City Hall building. Sharp still hadn't arrived.

The three men were workers known as "roustabouts" in circus and carnie environments. Basically, they did whatever dirty job was assigned to them.

"You are three of the biggest men on the grounds," the Count said to them.

The three men stared at him blankly, as they had been hired for their brawn, not their brains.

"There's a man in town known as the Gunsmith," the Count said. "Have you heard of him?"

"Yeah, boss," one of them said.

"Well, he's been asking questions about me, and I want him stopped."

"Stopped?" one of them asked.

The Count saw that he had to be plainer.

"I want him beat to a pulp, put on his horse and sent on his way."

"But . . . his gun, boss," one said.

"He won't shoot an unarmed man," the Count said. "You three will be unarmed. You'll beat him down with your fists, and nothing else. Is that understood? Beat him, do not kill him."

"Got it, boss," one said.

"Then go do it!" the Count snapped.

The roustabouts left.

"Are you sure this is what you want to do?" Curtis asked.

"He's not going to join my show," the Count said, "he's asking questions about me—according to *you*, among others—and I don't want him to be in any condition to join the Irishman's show. So yes, this is what I want done."

Curtis shrugged and left.

Chapter Forty-One

The three burly roustabouts may have been hired for their brawn and not their brains, but that didn't mean they were completely dumb. As they got outside the building, they stopped to huddle and talk.

"This is a dangerous fella," one said.

"We need more help," another said.

They all agreed that they would each draft another of the roustabouts, so that they would be six against one. Those were odds they each felt comfortable with.

Curtis came out and found them there.

"What's going on?" he demanded.

All three men looked startled when he appeared, and they were all uncomfortable around the little man.

"Just makin' plans," one said.

"What plans?" Curtis asked. "You don't have a brain among you. Just beat the man to a pulp!"

"Right!" one said, and they all slunk away.

Curtis shook his head. They may have been given size, but he had been given brains, and he actually preferred it that way.

***

The roustabouts collected their extra men, and the six of them went looking for the Gunsmith.

Meanwhile, they missed Clint when he walked Johnny Sharp to City Hall and watched the young man go in.

As Clint walked away, Sharp went into the Count's office.

"It's about time," the Count said.

"I don't like interrupting my target practice time," Sharp said.

"Take a seat," the Count said.

Sharp sat across from him, looking sullen. He was still thinking about what the Gunsmith had told him and wasn't sure he could question his mentor.

"You can stop worrying about the Gunsmith," the Count told him.

"Why?"

"Because I'm having him taken care of."

"So you ain't lookin' to sign him up, anymore?" Sharp asked.

"I don't need to sign a washed-up old gunslinger, Johnny," the Count said. "I have you."

"Whatayou mean?" Sharp asked.

"I mean he'll be gone soon."

"You ain't gonna kill 'im, are you?"

"What would make you ask a foolish question like that, Johnny?" the Count replied. "Why would I kill him? I'm just having him . . . removed."

"How?"

"Don't worry about it," the Count said. "Just know that you're my headliner and keep working on your skills. You're going to be the most popular sharpshooter since Annie Oakley, Johnny."

If the Count was determined to make that happen, Sharp wasn't going to ask him any of the questions Clint Adams had mentioned. Johnny Sharp was going to follow his mentor as far as the man wanted to take him.

"Yes, sir."

"Just stay away from Adams until it's all over," the Count said.

"And when will that be?" Sharp asked.

"Hopefully," the Count said, "by the end of today."

Excited, Sharp left the Count and went looking for the only person he wanted to brag to.

***

"He said what?"

"I'm gonna be the biggest thing since Annie Oakley," Sharp repeated.

"No, no," she said, waving his comments off, "what did you say before that?"

"Oh," Sharp replied, "he's havin' Clint Adams taken care of."

"How?"

"He didn't say," Sharp said. "He just told me to stay away from him and stop worrying about him, that he'd be taken care of by the end of the day."

Belle grabbed her shawl and tossed it over the shoulders of her beige dress.

"Where are you goin'?" Sharp asked, as she headed for the door. "I wanted to celebrate."

"You want to celebrate, Johnny?" she said. "Wait for the Count to come home and celebrate with him!"

She left the house, slamming the door behind her.

Sharp stood in the center of the Count's house, feeling baffled by Belle's response.

Belle ran down the street, bound and determined to find Clint Adams.

Chapter Forty-Two

After leaving Johnny Sharp at the City Hall building, Clint drifted away, thinking that his next move might have to be seeing the Count, himself. The man had probably heard by now that he was asking questions about him. Why not approach him with those questions directly?

There were only two places to spend time in Freakville—the big top or mess tent. In the big top the performers would be rehearsing, and he didn't want to bother them. There was the usual line of people waiting for food in the mess tent, so he went and poured himself a cup of coffee.

He sat at a table by himself and watched the freaks and oddities move about. Some of them sat together, laughed and talked, others sat alone, ate and brooded. Some were comfortable with who and what they were. Others resented it. He thought he knew how both sides felt.

He was finishing up his coffee when Belle came into the tent, looking harried. She spotted him and came rushing over.

"What's going on?" he asked, as she sat across from him.

"The Count is planning something," she said.

"What?"

"I don't know," she said, "but he told Johnny you probably wouldn't be a problem after tonight."

"What do you think he meant by that?"

"I don't know for sure," she said, "but I think it's something bad."

"Well," Clint said, "I was thinking about going and talking to him, so I guess this makes up my mind."

"Maybe you can talk him out of doing something stupid."

"Or evil?"

"Are you still thinking about what Kyra said?"

"I'm still thinking about Kyra, yeah."

"Maybe you should be thinking about me," Belle said.

"You creep into my thoughts from time to time," Clint admitted.

"Well, then I'm flattered."

"Thanks for warning me," he said. "I'll be on the lookout for trouble. By the way, you didn't happen to locate that letter we talked about, did you?"

"Not yet," she said, "I'm still looking."

"Thanks."

"Okay," she said, "my job's done. But while I'm here, I might as well have something to eat."

"Do you often eat in here with everybody else?" he asked. "I thought you ate with the Count."

"I never eat with the Count," she said, standing up. "He insists on eating alone."

"Is he at the City Hall building now?"

"Probably."

Clint stood up.

"Now's as good a time as any. I'll see you later."

Belle went and got in line while Clint left the tent.

***

When he reached City Hall, he went right inside to the Count's office and entered without knocking. The man's head jerked up from his desktop.

"Usually people knock," the Count said, sitting back in his chair.

"You and me need to talk," Clint said.

"About my offer?" the Count asked. "I've changed my mind. I don't need you. Johnny's my headliner."

"That's good," Clint said. "He's a talented kid."

"Yes, he is," the Count said. "I never should have thought about replacing him. I don't need you."

"That's not why I'm here," Clint said.

"Then why *are* you here?"

"I heard you were planning something," Clint said.

"I'm planning a lot of things," the Count said. He spread his arms over the mess of papers on his desk. "That's what this is all about."

"No," Clint said, "I mean, something about me. I heard you said I wouldn't be a problem after tonight."

"If I did say that," the Count replied, "it's only because I thought you'd be leaving us come morning."

"And why would you think that?"

"I told you," the Count said. "We don't need you. I was going to find you today and tell you that."

"I see."

"What did you think I meant?" the Count asked. "That I was going to try to hurt you?"

"I don't know," Clint said. "Maybe."

"Look," the Count said, "I don't care what you heard, Mr. Adams, but I'm not a bad man."

"I wish I could believe that," Clint said.

"Why can't you?"

"A lot of people here are afraid of you."

The Count leaned forward, set his elbows down on the desk.

"If that's the case," he said, "then why are they still here?"

"I think a lot of them feel they have nowhere else to go," Clint said.

"Look," the Count said, "all of the people who are here now are welcome. I don't know if I'll be able to use all of them in my show, but that's a decision for later. If they're in fear, maybe it's because they soon may not have a job."

"Maybe that's it," Clint said. "As far as you not being a bad man, I guess that still remains to be seen."

"If we're finished here," the Count said, "I have a lot of work to do."

"We're finished," Clint said, "for now," and left.

***

Curtis tracked down two of the roustabouts the Count had talked to.

"The Count sent me to find you," he lied. "There's been a change of plans."

"What'zat?" one asked.

"He doesn't want the Gunsmith to walk away from here."

"He wants us to kill 'im?"

"That's what he's thinking," Curtis lied again. "Is that a problem?"

"Well . . ."

"There's money in it for you."

The man narrowed his eyes and exchanged a glance with his partner.

"How much?"

"How many of you will there be?" Curtis asked.

"Six," the man said. "We recruited some extra help."

"All right, then," Curtis said, "let's talk money."

They not only talked money, but the whens and wheres. When Curtis left the two roustabouts to pass the information on to their partners, he was very satisfied with himself.

Chapter Forty-Three

When Clint left the Count, he didn't feel much in the way of satisfaction. He wasn't convinced that the Count wasn't plotting something against him, or that Kyra was wrong about the man. The Devil, no, but a bad, evil man—that was still up in the air.

He decided to broach the subject of the Count with the men he would be playing poker with that night, most likely Jack, Gordo, Lefty and Destro. One of them might have a helpful opinion.

Earlier, when he thought there was only two places to spend time, he had forgotten about the secret saloon Jack had taken him to. Could be somebody there might have an opinion. In any case, he could get a beer.

As long as they let him in without Jack, or someone else to sponsor him.

"There was only one way to find out.

***

He found the place with no trouble and knocked on the door. When it was opened by the bartender he asked, "Okay, if I come in?"

"Sure thing, Mr. Adams," the man said. "Come ahead. Jack says you can use the place any time you like."

Clint entered, waited until the bartender closed and locked the door, then went to the bar with him. A couple of burly types sat at one table and looked up at him, curiously. A couple of others had seen him there before, and simply nodded.

"He's okay," the bartender told the two burlys, but they stood up and hurriedly left.

"Didn't mean to lose you any customers," he said to the bartender.

"Don't matter," the man said. "They're just roustabouts."

"Roustabouts?" Clint hadn't heard the word before.

"They do the dirty work," the bartender said. "Erect the tents, break them down, clean up, repairs, heavy liftin', whatever. You want a drink?"

"A beer, please."

"Comin' up."

He set a cold one down in front of Clint, who hoisted it and sipped gratefully.

"Thanks," he said. "I needed that."

"Let me know if ya need anythin' else."

"Well," Clint said, "now that you mention it . . ."

"Yeah?"

"How much do you know about the Count?"

The man frowned.

"Why do you wanna know?"

"I'm not certain he's got everyone's best interest at heart," Clint said. "I was wondering if anyone in town agrees with me."

"Well, I sure do," the bartender said. "He pretty much rules these people by fear."

"Are they afraid of him?" Clint asked. "Or are they afraid they won't get a spot in the show?"

"That's a good question," the man said. "I think the folks who come here aren't afraid of him, or they wouldn't be sneakin' around here. They know he don't want his performers drinkin'. But the rest, I think they're pretty much just afraid of him."

"I've been told he's evil," Clint said. "What do you think of that?"

"I think he's selfish, egotistical, mean . . . but evil?" He shook his head. "I dunno."

"In plain talk," Clint asked, "would you say he's a bad man?"

"Yeah," the bartender said, "bad would cover it."

Clint drained his glass and set it on the bar.

"Thanks for your honest opinions," Clint said.

"Come on back, any time."

***

The two burly roustabouts who left the saloon when Clint got there joined up with the other four.

"He was in the saloon," they told them. "We coulda taken him there."

"Curtis said to be careful where we do it," one of the others said. "Out of sight, and best if we do it at night. We just gotta wait a few more hours."

They all nodded their agreement.

Chapter Forty-Four

The poker game was once again in the big top tent. All the rehearsals were finished and a round table had been set-up in the center.

As Clint entered the tent, he saw the folks he had expected to see already seated at the table: Smilin' Jack, Destro, Lefty and Gordo.

"The gang's all here," he said, taking a seat, "except Raza. He thinks Allah doesn't want him to play, anymore, since you told him about his tell."

"We're anxious to see if he can put what we learned from you to good use," Jack said.

"If you can all control your tells," Clint said, "it should just come down to whoever has the best cards."

They cut to see who would deal first, and Destro showed an Ace of Spades.

"If I didn't know better . . ." Lefty growled, showing his deuce.

"You know I don't use magic in a poker game," Destro told him.

"Yeah, yeah," Lefty said. "Deal the cards."

The already grumpy juggler was happier after he won the first hand.

Late into the night several burly roustabouts came in and started to move things around. Clint assumed they were either cleaning up or setting up for the next day's rehearsals—or both. He thought he recognized two of them from the saloon.

The game went on and Clint was impressed that the players all had their tells in check. He was still able to read some of them, but they didn't seem able to read each other. Money moved back and forth across the table, with most of it stopping in front of Clint, but the others didn't mind.

"So what did you decide, Clint?" Jack asked. "You leavin' us tomorrow?"

"I haven't really gotten the answers I was looking for, but I've assured Johnny I'm not after his spot in the show," Clint said.

"What answers were you lookin' for?" Destro asked.

"I want to know what the Count's planning," Clint said. "Is he just trying to put together a show to compete with the Irishman, or is there some selfish, and maybe evil reason behind it."

"I don't know about evil," the magician said, "but I'd vote for selfish."

"He's just tryin' to feed his ego," Lefty said.

"If I knew that was it, I'd be out of here," Clint said. "I don't care about his ego, I just don't want him hurting anybody."

"He's gonna hurt whoever he doesn't use in the show," Lefty said. "They're gonna be left out in the cold."

"That's show business," Gordo said.

They all looked at him.

"Well it is," the bronze-skinned strongman said.

"What do you think the Count is planning?" Lefty asked.

"I don't know," Clint said. "I just know I don't like him. And somebody told me he's got evil intentions."

"Oh," Destro said, "you've been talking to Kyra."

"Really?" Gordo said, looking interested. "Kyra don't talk to nobody."

"That's exactly why I put some confidence in what she says," Clint commented. "Because she came to me with it."

"So you don't know if you're leavin' or not?" Destro asked.

"Not sure, no," Clint said, "but the Count seems to think I am."

"How so?" Jack asked.

"Belle told me he said I wouldn't be a problem after tonight."

"That could mean anythin'," Lefty said.

"I know," Clint said.

They finished the game and Clint was glad to see he wasn't the only one showing a profit. Jack had also won.

Lefty and Destro said goodnight, while Clint and Jack counted their winnings and Gordo collected the cards. They had used several decks and he re-assembled them all. Then he said good-night and took the cards with him.

That left Clint and Jack in the tent, with several roustabouts still moving things around. In fact, it seemed to Clint they had simply moved things from one end of the tent to the other, and then back again.

"Jack," Clint said, "I think you better get going."

"The saloon for a drink?" the rubber-faced man asked.

"Sure," Clint said, I'll meet you there."

Jack nodded, picked up his money and left.

The roustabouts abandoned their makeshift chores and approached the table.

"What's going on, fellas?" Clint asked.

Three men faced him, and he noticed three more slip into the tent, which was fairly well lit by torches. All six men were large and casting long shadows.

"You know," Clint said, "the Count should've sent more than six of you. I can take care of six with my gun."

"You ain't gonna kill no unarmed men," one of them said.

"You're pretty sure of that, are you?" Clint asked, assuming this one was the leader.

"That's what we was told."

"And what else were you told?" Clint asked. "Maim me, or kill me?"

"Whatayou think?" the leader said.

Chapter Forty-Five

They were right. Clint didn't shoot unarmed men, but with these six he might not have a choice. Perhaps if he shot one of them it would head off a beating, or worse.

"What's goin' on?"

They all looked toward the entrance of the tent and saw Gordo standing there, looking puzzled.

"Get out of here, strong man," the leader said. "We got a job to do."

"What job?"

"They've been sent to kill me, Gordo," Clint said.

"What?" Gordo said. "This ain't right. Six against one ain't fair."

"Gordo," the leader hissed, "get lost!"

"You want me to go, Mr. Adams?" Gordo asked.

"Not really, Gordo," Clint said. "I kind of like having you here."

"You don't hafta shoot these fellas, ya know," Gordo said, moving further into the tent. "Jack told me you might need some help. I think you and me can handle 'em."

The leader laughed.

"You think six-against-two's gonna make a differ-ence?"

"Sure it is," Gordo said, with a smile Clint had never seen before, " 'cause now *we* got *you* outnumbered."

"You asked for this, big man," the leader said.

The three roustabouts behind Clint turned to greet Gordo, while the three in front of him advanced. He still considered shooting one of them but put that off until he could see what Gordo's presence would bring.

As the three roustabouts charged Gordo, the big strong man stood his ground until they were close enough, then exploded at them with his arms spread. They were three big men, but not as big as Gordo was. He slammed into them and took the three of them off their feet. Then, one-by-one, he grabbed them by the hair, lifted their heads and slammed a ham-sized fist into their faces. One, two, three times, and all three men were unconscious.

Clint had not even commenced his battle with his three yet when Gordo came and stood next to him.

"Relax," he told Clint, "I got this."

As Clint watched, the big strong man waded in, fists flashing. The roustabouts got in some shots, but they didn't seem to even make Gordo blink.

Clint was amazed by the big man's speed and his ability to withstand the blows tossed at him that did land.

The roustabouts were big, strong men, but he handled them like a man among boys. When the battle was done, there were six men lying on the ground, bloody and beaten. Gordo stood there, his shirt torn and bloody, only it wasn't his blood.

Gordo turned to Clint and asked, "What was that about?"

"Why don't we wake one of these guys up," Clint said, "and ask him?"

Gordo grabbed the leader by the collar, dragged him over to a barrel of water in a corner, and dunked his head in it. When he pulled him up, the man was sputtering and choking. Gordo dropped him to the ground.

"He's awake," he said, and proceeded to wash the blood off himself.

"What's your name?" Clint asked the man.

"Devlin," the man said, wiping the water from his eyes.

"What was this about, Devlin?" Clint asked. "Who sent you after me?"

Devlin hesitated, but Gordo growled, "Answer the man!"

"The Count told three of us to give you a goin' over," Devlin said. "Just to make sure, we recruited three more."

"So you weren't going to kill me?"

"Well . . . Curtis came to us later and said the Count changed his mind, he wanted you dead. He offered us money to kill you."

Clint looked at Gordo.

"The Count would need all the money he's got to launch his show," Clint said. "Why would he offer to pay to have me killed?"

"Maybe he's the evil man you been told he was," Gordo suggested.

"Yeah," Clint said, "maybe. Or maybe he's not the one who wanted me dead."

"Curtis?" Gordo asked.

"I've had the feeling Curtis has his own agenda," Clint said. He saw Gordo frown, so he added, "His own plans."

"You want me to find him for ya?" Gordo asked.

"Yeah, but in the morning," Clint said. "Bring him here in the morning. Meanwhile, let's tuck these six in for the night. Can you get some rope?"

"Lots of it," Gordo said.

"Tie the six of them up, gag them, and leave them in here," Clint said. "We'll spring them on Curtis in the morning and see how he reacts."

"Okay. Anything else?"

"Yeah, but I'll take care of it," Clint said. "I want the Count here, as well."

"How are you gonna arrange that?"

"I think Belle might be able to help."

Chapter Forty-Six

Clint was waiting in the big top tent the next morning, early. He had invited several people and was waiting for them to arrive.

Belle got there first.

"Did you talk to the Count?" he asked.

"He'll be here," she said. "I told him there was an emergency."

"Good."

"What's going on, Clint?" she asked. She was wearing a simple pink cotton dress this morning, with a shawl that she held tight.

"That's what I'm hoping to find out," he said.

Moments later the Count came striding in, blinked several times when he saw Clint, then looked at Belle.

"What's this about?" he asked.

"Ask Clint," she said. "It's his show."

The Count looked at Clint.'

"Are you surprised to see me in one piece, this morning?" Clint asked.

"What are you talking about?"

Clint walked over to where a tarpaulin was covering something, grabbed the edge of it and pulled it away. The six men who were tied up beneath it squinted and looked around.

"These men said you sent them to kill me last night," Clint said. "Thanks to Gordo, they failed."

"What? Kill?" the Count asked, surprised. "I never told them to kill you."

Clint reached down and removed the gag from Devlin's mouth.

"Boss," he croaked, then cleared his throat. "Curtis told us you want Adams dead, and that you were gonna pay us."

"What the—" the Count started, but at that moment they heard some screeching from outside. Moments later, Gordo walked in with Curtis slung over his shoulder.

"Put me doooooown!" Curtis was yelling.

Gordo unceremoniously dumped Curtis on the ground with a thud.

"Ow!" the little man shouted. "What the hell—"

"Curtis," the Count said, "did you tell these men I wanted Adams killed?"

The little man stared up at him,

"That's what you told me."

"No, it's not!" the Count snapped.

"Well, maybe I misunderstood."

"I don't think you misunderstood anything," Clint said. "Why do you want me dead, Curtis?"

"Answer him!" the Count shouted.

"You weren't going to join the show," Curtis said. "I have a lot of money invested here." He looked at the Count. "Do you know the kind of publicity we would get if the Gunsmith was killed here?"

"Money?" Clint said. "What money?" He looked at the Count. "What's he talking about?"

"Curtis is my partner," the Count said.

"He's the evil one!"

They looked at the tent entrance and saw Kyra standing there, pointing at Curtis.

"He's the evil I've been feeling."

They all stared down at Curtis.

"Hey," he said, "I'm just trying to make money!"

***

They released the six roustabouts and sent them back to work. They had orders never to talk to Curtis, again.

Belle moved out of the Count's house later that day. In fact, she said she was leaving Freakville.

"How?" Clint asked. "You don't have a horse."

"I'll figure out a way," she said. "And oh, I never did find that letter."

"You know what?" Clint said. "It doesn't matter what his real name is. Without Curtis there may never be a show."

"Well," she said, "the other freaks here are going to stick with him."

They were sitting in the mess tent, drinking coffee and saying goodbye. Clint looked around. Everything looked normal.

"Even Gordo?" Clint asked her.

"Yes," she said. "He doesn't know where else to go."

"He saved my life," Clint said. "Or, at the very least, saved me from taking a life. I wish I could help him."

They stood up and left the tent. Clint's Tobiano was outside, packed and ready to go.

"Thank you for all you did," she said, kissing his cheek. "You showed me the Count isn't infallible, and that gave me the courage to leave."

She turned and walked away. Clint was about to mount up when he saw Kyra coming from the other direction. He still didn't know if his night with her in Flagstaff was a dream or not.

He turned to face her.

"Leaving?" she asked.

"I can't do any more here," he said.

"You did enough," she said. "You found the evil."

"Will you be staying here?" he asked.

"Who knows?" she said. "I go like the wind."

"What's that mean?"

She smiled, went to him, pressed her cheek to his and her mouth to his ear.

"Maybe we'll have another night together sometime," she whispered. "Who knows?"

She laughed, turned and ran off, her laughter echoing in his head.

Coming September 27, 2021

THE GUNSMITH
474
OUTLAW'S GUN

For more information
visit: www.SpeakingVolumes.us

On Sale Now!

THE GUNSMITH *series*
Books 430 – 472

**For more information
visit:** www.SpeakingVolumes.us

On Sale Now!

THE GUNSMITH GIANT *series*

**For more information
visit:** www.SpeakingVolumes.us

On Sale Now!

Lady Gunsmith *series*
Books 1 - 9
Roxy Doyle and the Lady Executioner

For more information
visit: www.SpeakingVolumes.us

On Sale Now!

TALBOT ROPER NOVELS
by
ROBERT J. RANDISI

For more information
visit: www.SpeakingVolumes.us

On Sale Now!

Award-Winning Author
Robert J. Randisi (J.R. Roberts)

For more information
visit: www.SpeakingVolumes.us

Sign up for free and bargain books

Join the Speaking Volumes
mailing list

Text
ILOVEBOOKS
to 22828 to get started.

Message and data rates may apply.

www.ingramcontent.com/pod-product-compliance
Lightning Source LLC
Chambersburg PA
CBHW032048240626
47154CB00003B/1129